Hastings
Security 4

Not
THE BODYGUARD'S
Princess

LORIN GRACE

CURRANT
CREEK PRESS

Cover Design © 2019 Evan Frederickson and LJP Creative Graphics
Photos © iStock

Formatting by LJP Creative
Edits by Eschler Editing

Published by Currant Creek Press
North Logan, Utah
Not the Bodyguard's Princess© 2020 by Lorin Grace

First edition: July 2020
ISBN: 978-1-970148-09-1

to Snoopy

MY LAPTOP IS JEALOUS OF YOU TOO

"Idiots."

Jordan peered through the small plane's window at the gathering crowd and instantly agreed with Blake. "How did they know I'd be here? Hearthfire promised to keep my arrival quiet."

They'd chosen the municipal airport north of Green Bay for its remote location. The entire point of taking the private jet had been to avoid the chaotic scene now unfolding at the side of the tarmac. Judging by the satellites on top of two vehicles, at least two local television stations had joined the throng of fans.

"The channel needs more publicity." The graying bodyguard who'd watched over her for all her twenty-six years was rarely wrong.

"They could have warned us." At least she'd changed from the yoga pants and oversized shirt she'd boarded the plane with to jeans and a green sweater. "Too bad it isn't a blustery fall day. No one likes having the wind toss airplane dust in their face."

"I see three bodyguards from the studio over by the crowd. Stu is with the producer." Disdain filled Blake's voice. There was little love lost between Jordan's personal bodyguard and the studio's lead bodyguard, Stu.

"Four bodyguards for a crowd of a hundred?" Jordan used a compact to check her makeup. Anything short of raccoon eyes, she'd live with.

"One hundred fifty and more arriving. I don't like the setup. Too few guards. Keep Princess with you. I need both hands free." He didn't need to say more. Under her updated contract, Hearthfire supplied their own bodyguards on the set and for public appearances, limiting Jordan's personal security. Blake often grumbled that most of the studio's guards had learned everything they knew at the movie set.

Jordan clipped a leash on her well-groomed mutt and slung a cross-body bag over her shoulder. She would have grabbed her carry-on too, but that would make waving at her fans difficult. Someone would get it to her hotel. "Ready, Princess?" The dog wagged her tail and tugged at the leash. Jordan hoped they could find a patch of grass soon, as her little dog had been good the entire flight.

Shouts of "Princess! Princess!" arose as they exited the plane. Her mutt wagged her tail and leapt with excitement. She petted her dog. "Calm down, they aren't here to see you." After her three and a half seasons playing Princess Sam, some fans no longer made the distinction between the actress and her adventurous character.

Paul, the producer, met her at the bottom of the stairway. Princess pulled at her leash, eager to reach the patch of grass near the fence. Jordan obliged. Better than getting caught in argument 436 between her bodyguard and her boss and producer about her safety. It didn't matter. She had no choice but to sign autographs and wave since Stu and Paul weren't taking any of the letters or threats seriously. Blake would try to keep her as safe as one man could. If only she had the rest of his team to guard her back.

Neither the chanting of the crowd nor the intensity of the argument had wound down by the time Jordan and Princess returned.

Blake stood with his arms crossed. "What do you mean there's no room for me at the hotel?"

"You are not a Hearthfire employee or contractor, and we are not obligated to make your accommodations. Now, we must get moving. Jordan's fans are waiting." The producer pulled out his phone and pointed to his scheduling app. "Stu, tell security we're coming."

"Wait. I have a two-room suite, don't I?" asked Jordan.

"Of course you do."

"Then Blake stays with me."

Paul used his most condescending smile, the one usually reserved for when an actor argued about their part. "How will it look to your fans, you sharing a room with a man twice your age? It violates your morality clause."

"One, my fans better not know where I'm staying, and two, I always have Blake with me, so it will look normal." The teen fans didn't worry Jordan. It was the adult males she was avoiding, especially since the recent escalation in gifts and letters over the summer.

"His presence at the hotel isn't in your contract. There's another hotel across the street. Now, hurry yourself over to your fans before they mutiny and I hold you in breach of contract. Your bodyguard friend can take care of your dog."

Jordan glanced at Blake, who gave the tiniest shake of his head. "I'll keep Princess with me."

"No, give him the dog. I don't want complaints about that bag of fleas scaring your fans."

As if the well-groomed fifteen-pound ball of fur was even remotely scary. However, many people had fears, and Jordan respected that. Jordan handed Blake Princess's leash.

Flanked by Paul and Stu, she went to meet the waving and cheering fans, Blake just behind her.

"Cute dog. What's her name?" asked a tall redheaded teen girl.

"Princess. She's a rescue."

"She looks like a fox."

A practiced laugh escaped Jordan's lips. "She is a dachshund-terrier mix, but don't tell her. She thinks it's cooler to be a fox."

The girl handed her a six-month-old tabloid. "Will you sign it? For my mom."

The process was repeated as Jordan walked toward the waiting black SUV.

Jordan stopped to sign a poster for a young teen in a wheelchair. "What's your name?"

"Her name is Hannah. She's deaf," said an adult female standing behind the teen, probably her mother.

Jordan signed to the teen. "Nice to meet you, Hannah. I'm happy you came today."

"You know ASL?" The girl bounced in her chair as she signed.

"Yes, I learned it for a movie when I was ten. My skills are poor, though." The sign she used for *poor* meant "unskilled" or "spastic" and was one of Jordan's favorites.

The girl turned to the woman behind her. "I'm right! She is in my movie," she signed with a huge grin.

"That movie is why I learned ASL. Thank you for watching it." Jordan autographed the poster and waved an *ILY* hand, the common *I love you* sign, before moving on to the next fan.

Several of them held posters asking, "Will the Princesses fall in love?" Others shouted questions about the film she couldn't answer. As she reached the end of the line of well-wishers, Blake moved to her side, separating her from her fans. As she turned to see why, a loud pop echoed above the cheering.

Blake tackled Jordan to the ground, Princess barked, and the fans screamed.

More pops. Two? Three? Jordan brought her hand to her head to find blood.

Blake didn't move from on top of her.

In the distance, sirens wailed.

Jordan blinked back the tears and prayed.

The happy birthday song was never intended to be whispered. Yet that's exactly what the entire Hastings family was doing, except for Andrew, who sang it in sign language. September covered her mouth to keep from laughing and waking up any of the five babies in the backyard, including her ten-month-old daughter snuggled in Adam's arms.

She leaned over and blew out all twenty-six candles, and the family air-clapped.

Andrew couldn't resist asking, "What did you wish for?"

"I know I'm not supposed to tell, but I wished that Adam will be happy since I'm officially accepting his proposal." September blushed and kissed the oldest Hastings brother on the cheek. Adam handed Andrew his sleeping soon to be daughter and grabbed September around the waist, dipping her into a picture-perfect kiss. No one was keeping their applause or joy silent now, their shouts and whistles filling the air. Abbie's triplets woke up in unison, which woke Alex's stepson. Only Harmony, who was gaining a father with the announcement, slept through the commotion, snuggled safely in Andrew's arms.

"Look, Andrew has the magic touch." September kissed the top of Harmony's head, careful not to wake her.

"Nah, he's just good at boring women to sleep." Adam nudged Andrew in the ribs. "How many dates have fallen asleep before the night was over?"

Alan joined in the fun. "Thirty-five or forty last time I checked."

"At least I go on dates." Andrew's comment earned a quick look from his mother, who rocked the triplet wearing green. "*Only* three. Like you've never had a date fall asleep during a movie. And one of them had mono. She fell asleep midsentence!"

Abbie rolled her eyes and patted the red-shirted triplet on the back. "Hey, guys, it's September's birthday, not pick-on-Andrew day."

"All days are pick-on-Andrew day." Alex's smile disarmed his statement. "It's what he gets for being the baby of the family."

"Careful, dear, there are little ears around, and we don't want them picking up any of your nonsense." Kimberly handed Alex a burp cloth. "Since most of them are destined to be older siblings, we don't need to set a precedent."

Too late. Andrew kept the comment to himself. He'd learned the quickest way to end the teasing was to not fight back. It wasn't like he was the only unmarried Hastings sibling. Alan hadn't dated since last summer.

"I say we cut the cake." Jethro Hastings set a bucket of ice cream on the picnic table, effectively ending his children's teasing. He handed September a slice of cake as her phone rang. She frowned before excusing herself and leaving her cake behind.

"Watch Harmony for us." Adam hurried after his fiancée, leaving the baby with Andrew.

Swiping a plate of cake and ice cream, Andrew headed for a chair on the far side of the porch. If he was lucky, he could finish it before Harmony woke up and reached for his food, though eating with a baby in his arms was a skill he'd honed over the last several months as his role of uncle grew. Harmony had recently learned that grown-up food tasted better than the mashed-up stuff she'd been eating. He was halfway through when September and Adam returned.

"September has an emergency she wants our help with. Listen up." Adam's usual shrill, attention-getting whistle was missing from the announcement. Having five babies in the family changed everything.

September gripped Adam's hand. "That phone call was from Jordan Lee. She's filming in Wisconsin for a Hearthfire movie I have a couple of scenes in. She's the actress I was in that teen musical with seven years ago."

"Isn't she the Princess?" asked Abbie.

"Yes, this is the series finale. Anyway, Jordan flew into a tiny airport a couple of hours ago, and someone took a shot at her. She's in the hospital now. Her personal bodyguard was injured, and she needs a replacement ASAP. She's met Adam and knows of Hastings. She asked me to bring someone up that she could hire. She sounds terrified."

Everyone turned to look at Andrew. With the recent reassignments due to Alex's switch to more office-based work, Andrew was the only brother available for full-time fieldwork.

"How big of a detail does she need?"

"Just one. Hearthfire has its own security team. The guard who got shot was the only personal guard with her. Adam, I think you've met him. He's been with Jordan forever."

Adam looked up from the phone he was consulting. "You mean Blake?"

"Yes."

Adam nodded. "Ya, I have. Good man. It's a three-hour drive to Green Bay. When should we leave?"

September studied her daughter. "If your mom will watch Harmony, now."

"Do you have a go-bag in your car?" Adam addressed the question to Andrew. Apparently it was a forgone conclusion that he would be taking this job, even though they hadn't even vetted the client.

"I have a three-day. How long would the job be?"

September consulted her phone. "Six-ish weeks. They are scheduled to wrap up the first week of November. Jordan said Blake took a bullet to the arm, shattering a bone. He's in surgery now."

"If we take this job, I'll need more clothes." Andrew's go-bag only held the basics. Hastings Security rarely took a job without meeting with the client or a thorough vetting by his father.

Adam put his arm around September. "September and I will be back and forth several times, so we can bring you anything else you need. Plus, Green Bay has stores."

Mom appeared, having divested herself of one grandchild only to pluck Harmony out of Andrew's arms. "I'll be happy to take care of this angel."

Andrew hugged everyone, then waved his farewells as he left the backyard, once again roped into a job with no one having asked his opinion.

THE NURSE CHECKED JORDAN'S VITALS one last time before exiting. Through the doorway, Jordan glimpsed a burgundy polo—one of the Hearthfire bodyguards stood just outside her door. Probably Stu. Where had he been when the shots were fired? He should have been the one to take her down. That was his job—or so Paul claimed. According to the police who had been asking questions earlier, the only ones seriously injured had been Blake and Jordan. The laceration she'd received requiring plastic surgery and the bump on her head weren't in the same category as Blake's gunshot wounds. Three bullets had hit him.

Jordan glanced at the clock. He'd been in surgery for nearly two hours. She closed her eyes and murmured another prayer, adding gratitude as only a few fans had suffered bumps and scrapes in ducking for cover. None of them had required a trip to the ER.

Stu knocked at the door as he opened it. "I thought you would like to know the police confirmed that the man Rod apprehended was the only shooter." Rod spent half of his time watching her rather than guarding her. It was a wonder he caught anyone.

"The detective told me." *Now leave*. She glared, hoping he would get the message.

Unfazed, Stu sat down in the chair closest to her bed. "I assume you would like to thank him for his quick thinking."

"Of course I do. But right now, I'm more concerned about Blake's surgery. Have you heard any news?"

Stu shifted in his seat. "No, I haven't."

Probably because he hadn't asked. "Grandma is very anxious about him. She asked me to call the second I know anything."

The announcement had its desired effect. Stu stood up. "I'll see if I can find anything out."

Jordan felt only slightly guilty lying. She hadn't spoken with her grandmother yet. Claire Lee was in India visiting one of her children's charities. The twelve-hour time difference made it sometime in the middle of the night there, and Grandma hadn't answered the text she'd sent. Their agent, Donetta, would try other methods of contacting her movie-star grandmother. Since Hearthfire films wanted Claire to appear in a cameo in the series finale, dropping her grandma's name was all Jordan needed to do to make any Hearthfire employee jump. Jordan didn't use the ploy often, but this afternoon, it seemed warranted.

Raised voices from the hallway caught her attention. Rod opened her door without knocking. Why didn't he understand there was a privacy line for bodyguards?

Wow, I'm irritable. The next face that appeared at the door helped smooth some of Jordan's emotions. The two faces behind September explained the raised voices. Jordan recognized Adam Hastings. The other had to be one of his brothers. The arrival of new personal security would annoy every man on Stu's team.

Rod blocked their path. "Ms. Platt is on your cleared list, but these two claim they need to come with her."

"I don't see a problem. They are her security, correct?"

Rod nodded but didn't move.

"September, come in and bring your bodyguards. Rod, let them pass."

"But I don't have them as cleared."

September tapped Rod on the shoulder. "You should. My contract specifies I will have my own security team, and I have been with Hastings Security for years. Now, can we pass, or shall I call Paul?"

Rod moved to the side as September entered with the Hastings men. The Hearthfire bodyguard stayed inside and closed the door.

"Rod, you don't need to be in here." Jordan tried to keep the irritation out of her voice while sounding firm.

Adam opened the door and waited. Something about his glare made Jordan want to leave the room too. Rod grunted and left.

"Thanks, Adam." Jordan turned to September. "I'm sorry to have called you away from your birthday party. But thanks for coming, and you guys too. I assume you are one of the famous Hastings brothers. All *A* names. I've heard so much about you. Mr. Alan, Mr. Alex, or Mr. Andrew?"

"I'm Andrew, er, Mr. Andrew." The younger guard extended his hand. Unlike Adam, he wore a navy polo with the Hastings logo above his heart. The handshake was light but firm, as if he was being overly careful not to hurt her.

"Don't be too annoyed if I forget the mister part of your name. September talks about the brothers all the time. Have a seat. I'm so glad you came." Jordan glanced at the door. It was more than likely that Rod was listening in. Rats. This would be easier if she could talk openly. Jordan sank into her pillow and closed her eyes, then opened them slowly. "It's been a long day. I hope someone will tell me about Blake's surgery soon. I still can't believe he took a bullet for me. He's been a part of my life since my first babyhood commercial. He always told me I'd be safe with him around, but I never thought he would prove it."

September reached over and held Jordan's hand. "I'm so sorry. Do you know anything?"

"Other than the bullets didn't hit anything that would kill him quickly, like an artery, no. I'm still trying to sort through what happened. Stu was next to me. He should have been the one protecting me, not Blake. Maybe Stu had protected Paul. I don't dare look at my phone to see what the news is saying. There were enough fans there. I'm sure some of them were live-streaming, plus the TV crews. I don't think I could watch. I only checked long enough to verify that Paul had told me the truth and that Blake and I were the only ones injured." Jordan wondered if she'd said the same thing twice.

September glanced at Adam, then quickly back. Too quickly. "Everything we have seen online confirms that. None of your fans were injured beyond a scrape or two."

But? "I'm so relieved."

"Fan injuries is one of my nightmares too." September gave her hand a squeeze. "I always feel safer with Adam around, even if he isn't officially on my detail."

A flash caught Jordan's eye. She pulled September's hand closer. "You're wearing a ring!"

"Yes, we made it official at my party. On the way up, we talked about getting married on Valentine's Day."

"I'd squeal, but I think it would make my head hurt worse." Jordan closed her eyes again and counted to ten before opening them. "I want to hire Hastings security."

Andrew studied the actress. Her brown hair was pulled back in a ponytail. In the videos from the morning's shooting it had hung several inches below her shoulders. Someone must have pulled it up in the process of patching up her injuries. The clean white bandage sat above amber eyes. It could be the pain meds or residual trauma, but something was off. She was too guarded. It was as if she was holding herself together by the force of her smile while her eyes darted to the door, where Rod stood on the other side. Miss Lee seemed to distrust the bodyguard. Good. Her instincts matched his. That boded well if she became their client.

"I need to replace Blake with someone he can trust. He liked Adam when September and I worked together. Your team impressed him. Even if this had happened in some other place in the world, you would have been my first call."

Adam stood behind September. "Where is the rest of Blake's team?"

"There isn't one. Just him. My last contract negotiations didn't go as well as we would have liked. Paul doesn't like having any spare bodyguards hanging around since Hearthfire provides their own security group. It took quite a bit of negotiating for them to make an exception for Blake. Even then they pull things like they did today, where they didn't rent him a room."

"Why?"

"Paul said our hotel is full but that there is one across the street. Not ideal, I get that. I'm rambling, aren't I ... Oh—Blake's team. He's the only one here."

"Do you know what hotel they chose?" asked Adam.

"No. Paul said it's an extended-stay. I guess they couldn't find any short-term condos. I assume they'll let Princess stay in the hotel."

She certainly thought of herself as a princess, not just as some-one who played one on TV. Andrew tried to give the actress a bit of leeway, as she'd been hit in the head and from the IV she was on pain killers too. "We can figure out which one."

September swiped through her phone. "They've booked two rooms for me for two nights later this week. Maybe I have a confirmation." September bit her lip. "There it is, and three nights next week in the same hotel. I bet this is the one." She handed her phone to Adam. "I guess they didn't get the memo saying I wanted to rent a house. I want Harmony with me."

Adam handed the phone back. "Staying in hotels makes it dif-ficult to guard a principal. I can't believe they didn't allow you a condo or other short-term rental."

"They are shooting part of the film on the grounds of some mansion. There's a guesthouse, but Storm Tordon is staying there."

September looked up at the mention of one of the hottest A-list young actors of the year. "Is he the male lead? You didn't tell me that."

"And you still didn't hear it from me. They made everyone sign nondisclosures. Even with the pain meds, I should have remembered that. But you would have known in a few days anyway, when you sign yours," Jordan said flatly.

"Aren't you excited to work with him?" asked September.

"Storm made them give me a contract addendum specifying which brand and flavor of mints I'm required to use prior to filming our kissing scenes. I wanted to counter, forbidding his new aftershave, Thunder, on the set, but Grandma and Donetta wouldn't let me. Have you smelled it? I swear I'll have to wear Vicks like policemen do around a dead body. I visited a high school to give an assembly in May and thought I would die of asphyxiation. Every single male must have been wearing Thunder. I can act, but there is no way I can create on-screen chemistry if I have to smell that garbage."

Andrew smiled. He'd been spritzed with the stuff while on a shopping detail last week and spent the rest of his shift counting the hours until he could shower and change and rid himself of the smell.

September covered her smile with one hand. "Does he really wear it?"

"I've only met him once, but he had it on. He wanted to spend an evening getting to know me. But when he insisted it be alone at his place, I refused. He has too much of a reputation to take that sort of risk. No, I'm not excited. Where were we?"

Andrew stepped into Miss Lee's line of vision. "We need to figure out the terms. It is unusual to do a job with no detail or backup."

"Terms? I don't know. Blake would. I know he had a plan and all. I didn't worry about that kind of stuff. I'm not even sure what his contract says."

Someone tapped on the door and waited a second before opening it. A doctor in green scrubs entered. "Miss Lee? Mr. Blake asked me to tell you when he was out of surgery. He is, and it was successful. I know you have questions; however, I'm not authorized to give you any details. I'm sure you understand."

Miss Lee sat up straighter in the bed. "When can I see him?"

"He should be in his room soon. I'll ask the nurse to find a wheelchair and take you up when he's ready."

"Thank you, doctor." Jordan's smile reached her eyes for the second time since they'd entered the room. The first time had been at September's marriage announcement.

The doctor left.

Miss Lee turned to Andrew. "I'll take you to talk to Blake. Will that do?"

Since there was only one answer to that question, Andrew nodded.

"I'll get a contract written up. It would go to your agent, wouldn't it?" asked Adam.

"Yes. I'll text September her information." Miss Lee reached for her phone, but the bedside table sat outside her reach. Andrew handed it to her. She smiled. The third genuine smile.

"It will be a pleasure working with you," said Andrew.

While she texted, her cell phone played a popular movie theme song from the fifties. "I need to take this. Can you give me some privacy? Hello, Grandma."

September and Adam beat Andrew to the door.

"One minute, Grandma," Jordan tapped the mute button. "Oh. For the contract, I'm not hiring you to guard me. You're guarding Princess, my dog."

PRICELESS. AS CLICHÉ AS THAT word was, it was the only word Jordan could find to describe the look on Andrew Hastings's face as he closed the door. He'd better not be allergic to dogs. Jordan closed her eyes. The drugs were playing with her brain. She took a deep breath before tapping the unmute button. Grandma would worry if she could hear the drugs in her voice. "Sorry about that. I needed to clear the room."

"It's good to hear your voice, bunny. Donetta reassured me you only had a scrape or two when she got ahold of me, but I needed to hear you. One can only trust an agent so far. How's Blake? What happened? Did they catch the shooter? Do you think it's your most recent stalker?" Only the smallest amount of static filled the space on Claire Lee's call from India.

"Slow down, Grandma. Blake just got out of surgery. I don't know any specifics. I don't know much about the shooting either. The police told me more than Paul and the Hearthfire bodyguards did. I was trying to hire a replacement for Blake when you called. But I may have blown it."

"Who? How?"

"Have you ever heard of Hastings Security out of Chicago? September Platt uses them."

"Is that Jethro and Melanie Hastings? They're still in the business? I hired them almost forty years ago when I performed in a stage production there."

"I believe so. I've been talking with two of the sons, Adam and Andrew. As they were leaving, Andrew said something about working with me, and one of the Hearthfire guards was outside the door, so I clarified that he would be guarding Princess. The look on his face is going in my laughter file." Jordan didn't need to explain about the gaff. Her grandmother was more than aware of the intricacies of her bodyguard situation.

"I assume someone from Hearthfire can hear you now?"

"They are standing on the other side of the hospital-room door."

"Wait, are you in the hospital?"

"Yes. When Blake took me to the ground, I hit my head hard. They want to watch me overnight. A plastic surgeon stitched, or rather, glued, me back together." Jordan hoped no one had told Grandma what the surgeon suspected. She hadn't been cut by hitting a rock. Rather, a bullet had grazed the side of her forehead. Her hospital stay probably had more to do with keeping her out of public access than it did her headache. "He took three bullets for me, Grandma." Tears threatened to choke off her words, her acting skills no longer covering up her feelings like they had the last few hours. Blake was more than a bodyguard. He'd been her surrogate father for years. Which might account for the relatively few dates and fewer boyfriends she'd had.

"Oh, sweetheart, I wish I was there. But it would take me at least two days to get there, and I'm due in London first."

"Don't cut your tour short because of me. I'm not injured badly, and I would feel guilty. September is here, and she is very helpful. I'm not alone."

"I know. But I'd rather be there with you."

"Thanks, Grandma. I don't know if I want you here. I'd probably worry more about you." Grandma Claire was the only family Jordan had left. No way would she put her in danger.

"I have my own bodyguards. Hearthfire isn't going to dictate security to Claire Lee." Grandma slipped into referring to herself in the third person as she often did when referring to her acting career.

"I can have one too. As soon as I clear up a little canine misunderstanding."

"I'm sure he's thrilled to know he's guarding Princess." Grandma's voice held a bit of humor. "You'll be in my prayers, bunny. Let me know as soon as you know more about Blake."

"I will, Grandma."

Jordan disconnected the call and texted September to let her know it was safe to return to the room.

Dog? Surely she couldn't mean he would be guarding the mutt the actress had toted around the last year. "Her emotional-support dog," claimed the media. Andrew followed September and Adam to the closest elevator. He waited until the doors closed and they were alone before talking. "Was she serious? Her dog?"

September stifled a giggle with her hand. "You probably didn't hear me complaining to Adam about the Hearthfire contract. Paul, the producer, decided he doesn't want independent personal security on-site. Fortunately, they wanted me bad enough they made an exception, but I can only have a team of two, not the usual four. I may or may not have claimed that not having a bodyguard caused me emotional distress and I couldn't sing." Understandable. Anyone who followed September's career the past two years knew how much damage one bad bodyguard could do. However, given her former bodyguard's plea deal, most people were blissfully unaware of the depth of betrayal September endured at his hands.

"Are you trying to tell me I'm really not guarding her dog?"

"On paper, I'm sure that is exactly your job. Blake took the bullet for her instead of one of the Hearthfire guards supposedly guarding her. The Hearthfire guard protected the producer. They should have had more bodyguards near Jordan to begin with." Adam voiced the disgust they'd all felt in reviewing the video clips.

When the elevator reached the main floor, the three searched for a secluded seating area. A small nook with three seats, a potted plant, and reasonable sight lines east of the main lobby gave them the privacy they needed.

Adam pulled out his phone. "Looks like Alan and Dad went over the footage we found online. They agree with my initial assessment. The shooter was aiming for Miss Lee's bodyguard. I also don't think the man in custody is the person who did the shooting. He was too close to the security member who took him down. Someone intent on a mass shooting or on killing Miss Lee would not stand next to security. It would've been smarter to be on top of one of the private hangars."

Andrew studied the same information on his phone. "September, do you know if Miss Lee has any active threats?"

"We don't discuss things like that. You guys know the drill. It's your job to contact the personal security of anyone I work with if a threat might include them. There's always somebody sending an odd email or letter to the agent, commenting too much on a post, or showing up too often at events. Talking about threats is just creepy," she said and shifted slightly toward Adam.

Andrew's oldest brother slipped an arm around his intended. He scanned the area. He hadn't been thinking about guarding September. Watching Adam proved that his brother wasn't actively guarding her either. Thanks to their own security, hospitals were secure places to begin with. Andrew chided himself for not being more aware of his surroundings just because he was with family.

September's phone pinged. "That's Jordan. She says she's off the phone and would like us to come back up."

A different Hearthfire security member met them at the door to Jordan's room, along with a man Andrew recognized from the video as the one on Jordan's far left when the shooting began.

"Ah, September, nice of you to come. I'm sure Jordan enjoyed your visit. She is indisposed at the moment, and I'm sorry to say she won't be able to see you again today."

"Paul, you know my security team? Hastings—out of Chicago." September raised a questioning brow. "Is the doctor in there?"

"No. But she doesn't want to see anyone." Paul moved to block the door.

September held up her phone. "That's odd. She sent me this text a minute ago: *Done with phone call. Come back.* Sounds like she wants to see me."

"But it wouldn't be in her best interest." Paul continued to block the door.

"She can determine that for herself." September sidestepped Paul and knocked a rhythm on the door before pushing it open.

Adam followed. The Hearthfire bodyguard grabbed him by the arm. "Not you, buddy."

September didn't turn around to face the men. Instead, she held the door and spoke to Jordan. "Do you mind if my fiancé and bodyguard come in?"

"You are engaged?" Paul's question drowned out Jordan's answer.

September smiled sweetly. "You can read about it on my website and, I'm sure, on half of social media. 'September's birthday wish comes true: engaged to her bodyguard.'" September swept her arm in an arc as if reading the words off a marquee. "Adam, Andrew?"

Andrew and his brother followed September into the room and closed the door behind them.

"Paul's out there?" asked Miss Lee.

September walked around the bed. "He probably has his ear pressed against the crack."

"Nonsense, he's commandeered a stethoscope and is listening that way." Miss Lee rolled her eyes.

"Really?" The question slipped from Andrew's lips.

"He's gotten even more micromanaging the past few months."

September sat down in the seat she'd vacated earlier. "Is that possible?"

"Yes. Take the whole 'the entire cast will stay in the hotel I choose' thing. Or the exclusion of personal bodyguards."

"Yikes. How do you deal with that?"

"My on-screen motto works. 'A princess will always find a way.' And in the situation with the bodyguards, I'm very annoyed about that. Which reminds me—I don't know what happened to Princess." Worry clouded Miss Lee's eyes. "I think someone told me they took her to a vet, but that's when we were down in the emergency room and I was more worried about Blake. I don't even know if she was hurt." She stared at Andrew as if the comment was directed only to him.

Andrew took a step closer to the bed. "What would you like me to do when I locate her?"

"If she is at a vet's you better leave her there until I get out of here. I don't know how she will react to you not being Blake. Princess is a fifteen-pound dog with a fifty-pound bark. So help the person she doesn't take a liking to, the entire world will know about it."

"Is she a good judge of people?" asked Adam.

"The best. I'm curious as to how she'll react to her new bodyguard." Miss Lee's smile reached her eyes for the fourth time that day.

Not something Andrew normally counted, but he was finding his new client difficult to read. A knock on the door interrupted his next thought.

A NURSE ENTERED THE ROOM with a wheelchair. "Mr. Blake is asking for you. The doctor feels that if you are up to seeing him, a visit would be beneficial."

Jordan tossed back the blanket, then yanked it back in place before the men saw her stylish hospital-issue gown in its full glory. "Guys, do you mind?"

Adam and Andrew gave duplicate nods and left.

Jordan waited until the door closed before swinging her legs over the side of the bed. The nurse produced a pair of gray slipper socks with more nonskid dots on them than a full-grown cheetah. A patient would be more likely to stick to the floor than fall in those socks.

The nurse also handed her a second hospital gown. "Wear this one like a robe. It helps some. I have a blanket for your lap."

Jordan settled into the chair and turned to September. "Face check. Be honest. Do I look like a train wreck? Is anyone's cellphone photo going to trend on Twitter?"

September dug through her purse and pulled out a pack of facial wipes. "I think the no-makeup look will work best. Your mascara is smudged, and the makeup is off most of your face.

May I?" September crouched down in front of Jordan and gently wiped away the remains of her makeup.

"Do I want to know how bad it is after having two men in my room for the past hour?"

September's melodic laugh burst out. "Adam's seen me looking worse than this. And Andrew has too. You're in a hospital. People expect a certain amount of messiness." She tossed the wipe in the garbage can and pulled out a hairbrush and removed the hair band from Jordan's ponytail. "I'll be careful near your bandage. Only women in daytime soaps look glamorous in hospitals. There. Not too messy and not overdone."

"I thought you Hollywood types would be more worried about looks," said the nurse.

"Not much more than any other woman who puts on jeans instead of pajama bottoms to go grocery shopping." September put everything back in her bag. "We worry more about people trying to snap a photo of us and the photo trending on social media."

"My grandmother won't leave the house without full makeup and hair done," said Jordan.

The nurse pushed the wheelchair into the hallway. "My grandma does the same thing."

Paul, Adam, Andrew, and a bodyguard she didn't recognize in a burgundy Hearthfire polo followed them down the hall. The nurse stopped. "I can only take one of you in. Miss Lee, who would you like to accompany you?"

Paul pushed in front of the others. "She'll take me."

The show's producer was her last choice. "Mr. Andrew." He needed to meet Blake.

"Who's Mr. Andrew?" asked the nurse.

"Me."

"Wait just a minute. I have to go." Paul stepped around the nurse and directly in front of the wheelchair.

"Sir, Mr. Blake specifically asked for Miss Lee. She's the only one I *have* to take. However, since I know you guys want her to have a bodyguard, I've allowed her to choose *one*. Now, if you will please move before I call hospital security."

"I have rights." Paul didn't budge.

"So do patients. And as an employee of this hospital, it's my obligation to uphold the patients' rights. Now, will you move, or do I call security?"

Paul stepped aside. "Jordan, you know you should let me see Mr. Blake."

"No, I don't. Last time I checked, Blake was in my personal employ, not yours." Jordan turned to get a better look at Andrew and gave him a nod, silently asking him to intervene.

"We are blocking the hallway. People are beginning to stare. I'm sure you don't need any bad publicity." Andrew waved Paul aside.

The nurse pushed the wheelchair around Paul and to the elevator.

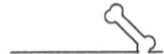

Blake, or Mr. Blake—Andrew wasn't clear if Blake was a first name or surname—raised the head of his bed as the nurse wheeled Miss Lee into the glass-walled room. A look of relief passed over the injured bodyguard's face, then was replaced by the same affectionate gaze Andrew's father had when looking at any of his sleeping grandchildren. The nurse slipped from the room and slid the glass door shut.

"I made a nuisance of myself and refused to take any pain meds until I saw you. I know the meds will help me recover, but I had to see you first." Blake reached the hand not in a sling out to Miss Lee. Andrew moved her chair closer.

"I've been so worried about you." Miss Lee leaned forward in her chair, trying to grab Blake's hand. She turned to Andrew. "Will you tell if I get out of this chair?"

"Not as long as you don't mind me standing close enough to catch you if you fall." Andrew set the brake on the chair and assisted Jordan to her feet, then pulled the chair out of her way so she wouldn't trip on it.

Blake focused on Andrew, squinting at the logo on his shirt. "You're one of Jethro's boys, aren't you? The ones with all the A names. The grade-A Hastings. Did she already hire you?"

Blake's use of the local nickname surprised Andrew. He assumed no one else knew outside of Chicago-area security companies. "I believe my job is to guard the dog."

Blake focused on Miss Lee. "Ears?"

"Not here. I don't think Paul could get onto the floor. But I have ears in my room."

"I guess I should call myself lucky to have ended up in one of these critical-care rooms. Doctor says they want me here overnight, and then they'll move me to another floor for a day or two." Blake focused on Andrew, the tightness in his face and jaw hinting at the pain he must be in. "If you think for one second this job is about the dog, I'll fire you on the spot."

"When Miss Lee first mentioned Princess, I was shocked. But after two interactions with Paul, I'm getting a better picture of what this job entails."

"Good. If it's a choice between the mutt and Jordan, I expect you to protect the human. Jordan can give you the contact information for my firm. We are small because Jordan and her grandmother are our only clients. Someone will fill you in on what you need to know. When I'm not under the influence of pain meds, I'll decide what happens next. I don't like that you are so young. But you are a Hastings, and your reputation is good enough. Had my Jordan contracted any other firm, I'd be on the phone rearranging things to get one of my regular contractors out here. Just promise me one thing, kid—you won't fall in love with my little girl. I've heard rumors about you Hastings, and I knew your parents back in the day. You have your family history against you on that one. She needs someone who will take a bullet for her, not the other way around."

Miss Lee's face reddened as Blake spoke. Andrew felt heat crawl up his own neck. He wasn't his older siblings. He would not fall for a client. Even if she was beautiful. Just because Abbie and Alex had married their clients didn't mean he would. Although, now, with Adam marrying September, the family's record for client relationships was in shambles.

"I wanted a full protection team, but Paul thwarted my efforts. I can only hope Hearthfire management will listen to reason after this incident and allow Jordan more security. I can't wait for Claire Lee to finish her work in India and be on set. Then I'll at least have a full crew here for a couple days." Blake closed his eyes and took a few shallow breaths, each one growing deeper than the last.

"Jordan, be as open in communicating with Andrew as you are with me. Probably more so as he isn't used to your communication codes. That is a language all your own. Now, if you'll push the red button for me, I'm ready for my pain meds." Taking a long, slow breath, Blake closed his eyes.

Jordan pushed the button, and Andrew hovered as she sat back down in the wheelchair.

A male nurse entered carrying a small tray with a syringe. "Here you go, Mr. Blake." He confirmed Mr. Blake's identity, which included his first name, Reginald, before sticking a needle into the IV port. The nurse turned to Miss Lee and Andrew. "Mr. Blake is likely to sleep for the next few hours. Shall I leave him a note to let you know if he would like visitors?"

"Yes, please," Jordan answered as her original nurse returned to take her back to the room.

"I can take her back." Andrew hoped the offer would give them a few minutes alone.

"Sorry, hospital policy. I already didn't interfere when you let her stand." The nurse's knit brows let him know she hadn't been pleased with the policy violation she'd easily viewed through the partially curtained windows.

As Andrew followed them to the elevator, questions about this job filled his head. He hoped a phone call to Blake's team would answer most of them.

Jordan handed him her open phone. "This is the number you need. Call it when you leave the hospital."

Andrew punched the number into his phone and handed hers back. Jordan hit the green dial button. "Hey, this is Jordan. I saw Blake. He approved Andrew Hastings for the interim. Mr. Andrew will call in an hour."

Miss Lee paused, then answered the next three questions with two yeses and a no before hanging up. "Sorry, I can't tell you more here."

The elevator doors opened. A Hearthfire guard waited across the hall for them. Ears.

THE DOCTOR SIGNED JORDAN'S RELEASE on Sunday afternoon. Stu had arranged for her to leave through an employee entrance at the back of the hospital to avoid the paparazzi. Unfortunately, he'd also accompanied her to say goodbye to Blake, who was now in a standard room, denying them any meaningful conversation.

Jordan texted Andrew from the car. **Going to hotel now. Can't wait to see Princess.**

—She's eager to see you too. The text included a photo of her dog curled up and asleep in a chair. To her surprise, he'd checked Princess out from the veterinary hospital last night and the two were getting along.

Stu and Paul followed her to her room, where Paul handed her a key card. The thought crossed her mind that he most likely had a duplicate. Oh, how she wished Blake were here. She waited for Stu to make sure the suite was clear before entering. Paul tried to follow her in.

Jordan put up a hand. "Not now, please. I still have a headache." Or she would if she had to talk to him for long.

"But we need to talk about Tuesday."

"We are doing a read-through, right?"

"Yes—"

"Has the script changed?"

"No, but I want to make sure you're ready."

"I'm sure I will be. With Monday to rest up, I'll be fine. I've been doing read-throughs for twenty years. I've played the role of Princess Sam for three and a half of those. Trust me, I'll be ready." She didn't try to disguise her sarcasm.

The elevator at the end of the hall pinged, and Andrew appeared with Princess on her leash.

"Besides, Princess hasn't seen me for over twenty-four hours. You don't want to see how hyper she can be."

Princess strained at her leash, and Andrew scooped her up. "Here you go—a princess for a princess."

Jordan ignored his lame joke and motioned him in, shutting the door on Stu's and Paul's frowning faces. "Let me sit down before you let Princess go. She'll greet me like I've been lost at sea for months."

Andrew did as asked. Jordan gave him a nod, and Princess bounded across the room and alternated between wanting to greet Jordan with a well-fended-off kiss and receiving a belly rub. Andrew opened his backpack, took out a small device, and slipped it on the back of his phone. He then made a slow circle of the main room. Typical for a hotel suite—a couch, most likely a fold out, a couple of chairs, and a coffee table built to outlive groups of frat boys. The television was bolted to a wall with something that would withstand a tornado. A desk with several generations of computer ports stood off to the side. Andrew stepped through the sliding glass doors to the balcony, slowly looking around and inspecting the locks.

Jordan had seen Blake do the same hundreds of times looking for cameras and bugs. Princess licked the back of Jordan's hand, demanding attention.

"Oh, sweet dog. Were you hurt yesterday or just scared?"

"The vet I spoke to said they didn't find any injuries. I'm not sure how Blake kept her from running when the shooting started."

Andrew circled the round table and chairs. He checked the hideous faux-silk flower centerpiece twice before rounding the corner into the galley kitchen.

"Carabiner. He always clips Princess to his belt with a retractable strap, then he doesn't have to worry about losing her. She jogs with him in the mornings, so she is used to keeping up with him if he has to run."

Andrew felt behind the TV and showed her a small device about the size of a pea before going over the room a second time. "September says you know ASL."

"A little." Jordan scratched under Princess's chin.

Andrew held up another pea-sized device. "How did you learn?"

"I was in a Helen Keller contemporary remix. It didn't do well."

"I saw you signing to a teen girl in the video footage from yesterday. You've kept up your skills." He checked the desk drawers.

"I guess it was something fun to do. Every once in a while it comes in handy. I don't practice enough." Princess poked her nose under Jordan's arm to inform her she had stopped scratching the dog's ears.

"What other skills have you learned for your movies?" Andrew pulled out a black bag and dropped the two devices in it. He signed, "Searching other rooms. Keep talking." He disappeared into the smaller of the bedrooms.

"I learned all the normal acting stuff—cry on cue, fall down, jump into a pit of foam. Some French, German, medical terms, that sort of thing." Jordan set the dog on the floor and followed Andrew. The room held twin beds. Not the one she would be using.

Andrew held up another device before dropping it into the bag. "Favorite role?"

"That is hard. I've loved some of my parts at the time and hated them later. I enjoyed acting so much as a little girl that for a long time it was like this game. Then I had a director who was harsh and yelled all the time, and the magic was gone. Grandma pulled me from that show. I've been very lucky that she oversaw my career. She started acting at twelve and has seen it all. Dad never enjoyed acting, so he didn't get it. I think he just did a few spots as a teen. He never wanted to be a TV doctor, just a real one."

Andrew paused in his search and looked at her. "Head hurt?" he signed as he crossed to the larger bedroom.

Jordan shook her head and sat down on the king-sized bed. Decent mattress. Good thing since she would be sleeping on it for the next six weeks. "Anyway, my favorite role at age five was one where I had a bunch of puppies on the set. I was so disappointed when they weren't going to be mine. Grandma bought me one from the trainer at the end of shooting. When I was around twelve, I played a witch—a good witch, of course. That was the first time I worked with green screens and wires and flying stunts. That was just fun. Ever since I turned sixteen, I've always been cast as the girl who gets the boy. Those aren't so much fun. I prefer musicals and supporting roles."

"Last one, I hope," signed Andrew coming out of the large bathroom. Then he signed something she didn't understand.

"Again?" she signed.

This time Andrew signed slower. "I found four b-u-g-s. Are there usually that many?"

"Not until the last three months," she signed back.

Andrew put the black bag in his backpack and spoke aloud. "I think Princess could use a walk. I found a dog park. Would you like to come?"

Princess's ears pricked at the words "dog park." She ran around Andrew's feet.

Did he know the Hearthfire guards would be following them if they made it out of the building? Or maybe that was his plan. "Sure. Let me grab my jacket."

32

They made it two blocks before Andrew picked out the rented SUV following them. Not a good response time on Hearthfire's part. Andrew expected to see the Hearthfire guards before he and Jordan had exited the elevator. The fact that they'd made it two blocks in a car unnoticed was worrisome.

Miss Lee's phone rang.

"Paul. Should I answer it?" Miss Lee held out her phone.

"Yes."

Miss Lee answered on speaker. "Hello, Paul."

"Where are you going?"

"Taking Princess to a dog park." Jordan crossed her eyes.

Assuming the bugs belonged to Hearthfire, Andrew must have gotten them all, or they wouldn't have needed to ask. Or the bugs were someone else's. Like an unethical paparazzi member or an unknown threat.

"Without any bodyguards?" Paul's voice grew louder.

"Andrew Hastings is with me."

"He isn't your bodyguard."

"I'm not working at the moment."

"Your safety on location is our responsibility." Too bad Paul hadn't thought about that yesterday before setting up the media at the airport.

"It's late Sunday afternoon at a dog park. I think Mr. Andrew can watch me play with Princess. And keep any old ladies in the area from pestering me."

"Stu and his team are following you. Wait for them before getting out of the car and don't pull this stunt again." The line went dead, and Jordan put the phone away.

Paul wasn't in the SUV. Good to know, he was micromanaging but not into doing the work himself. Andrew took the next left, sending the GPS into panic take-a-U-turn mode. "Do you mind if I take the most scenic route? I want to talk, and I'm sure my car isn't bugged."

"Do you think the bugs in my room were from Paul?"

33

"Possibly. Their response time for knowing you'd left the building was slower than I anticipated." If the security team had been using the bugs to watch her, they hadn't monitored them well.

"They don't track me like Blake does. He knows I'm going to sneeze before I do. Did Blake's team give you their app?"

"Yes. I downloaded it last night. The same company that designed ours designed it." The Hasting's app had more bells and whistles than Blake's, which was to be expected considering the designer was a Hastings's client.

"Then you are more likely to know where I am than Hearthfire is. They don't use any apps. My panic word is *aglet*."

"Interesting choice."

"I chose it years ago because Blake didn't know what it meant. I thought I was so smart."

Andrew chuckled and turned another corner. "I remember using *aglet* in a sentence for the first time, and I was disappointed when everyone in my family already knew the word. But I rarely know anything first."

"You're the youngest, aren't you?"

"Yes. And no one lets me forget it."

"I've wondered what having siblings would be like in real life. Many of my early roles were as the little sister in the family. But then I had all the funny lines. I assume that isn't the way it is in real families."

"I never had the witty lines. Those went to the twins. I used to pretend I was their triplet." Andrew took another left. "It didn't work out so well. Not that they were mean or anything, but they have a level of communication I've never shared." Miss Lee was easy to talk to, and he was talking too much. He'd taken this detour to get some things covered without prying ears. Andrew changed subjects. "I have a first-floor room at the hotel. As far as Princess is concerned, it's ideal as it has a door that leads directly to a three-by-five-foot patch of grass. I'm close to the stairwell, so I can get to your third-floor room fairly fast—not as fast as I'd like, but faster than if I was across the street."

"I thought the hotel was full."

"September had a reservation for two rooms on the days she was in for the shooting and pulled some strings. She rented a house yesterday before returning home." It hadn't been quite that easy, but Miss Lee didn't need to know the particulars. Fortunately, Mr. Blake's crew had deep pockets and had paid to have a guest moved to a sister hotel for an upgrade.

"I'm glad. Did Blake's people tell you about the threats I've received? And about their suspicions?"

"The ones starting in May after this new bodyguard policy?"

She nodded. According to the woman he'd spoken with, the threats were mostly notes left in places people shouldn't have been able to access, like her dressing room and trailer, but Stu didn't think the threats were a security issue. Last month, part of her wardrobe had disappeared.

"Good, I didn't want to have to explain what I know. Which, knowing Blake, isn't everything."

"Why did Hearthfire start the no-personal-security policy?"

"Paul is insisting on it. Maybe it has to do with Storm's contract."

Andrew took another turn into a cul-de-sac, his exit taking him past Stu's SUV. "What do you know about the threats?"

"You should ask Blake's wife. She's the team's secretary and keeps the files. Is she flying out? I didn't think to ask Blake."

"I didn't ask him either. What's Blake's routine? How often is he with you?" Andrew needed more information about this job.

"Hearthfire lets him on the set and things but not all the time. If Princess can be there, Blake can be in the room. We went to the trouble of registering her as an emotional-support animal so I can claim I need her. Don't lecture me about abusing the system. I don't take her shopping or out to restaurants or things like that. She isn't a service animal."

Andrew hadn't been on a movie-production set, just on talk shows and stage productions. Tonight, he would ask Adam for pointers. "What about this week's schedule?"

"We are doing a read-through Tuesday in the hotel conference room. I know Paul won't allow you in there. Only principal actors and the director—no dog unless I beg. For the biweekly show, Blake got Paul to let him stay when they closed the set. I'm worried you won't get the same exemption."

"I've thought about that. I'll go visit Blake tomorrow. There is a second read-through later this week, isn't there?"

"Yes. Paul only wants the principals there for Tuesday's. He is worried about how Storm and I will work together since I refused to meet with Storm in LA. Apparently I'm the only woman between sixteen and forty-five who doesn't swoon when the man walks in. Maybe I'm immune to the effects of Thunder."

Andrew turned another corner and checked his rearview mirror. Stu sat on his tail, not even hiding the fact that he was following them. "How much do you know about the bodyguard who took down the shooter?"

"Rod? Not much. He's quiet and spends more time than he should staring at me. Slightly creepy. To be honest, I'm surprised he tackled the shooter. Not to be rude... Rod follows orders well, but he is a can or two short of a six-pack. Why?"

"Mostly curious." Andrew held an internal debate before continuing. In the videos, Rod had stood too close to the shooter to have allowed three shots. One clip thirty seconds before the shooting showed the two men only five feet apart. Sadly, no one seemed to have caught the actual shooting on camera. Alan insisted all of the bullets were meant for Blake but without more footage, he couldn't prove his theory. Footage the police didn't seem to have either. "What about the other guards? Do any of them act strange?"

Jordan looked over her shoulder at the car tailing them. "Stu looks angry. According to Blake, other than Stu, they're all incompetent. They blame me for things all the time. Stu's a better bodyguard than team leader."

"Do you have any questions for me?" Andrew tried a different tactic. He needed more information, and he needed her trust.

Jordan stared out the window for a moment. "Where did you learn to sign?"

"I took ASL in high school, then continued in college. I have an interpreter's license, but I don't use it much. ASL comes in handy when Hastings is hired to protect out-of-town actors for *Children of a Lesser God* or other productions."

"Blake and I use some of our own signs to communicate when we need to around Paul and Stu. If I think I'm in trouble, I sign 'shoes.' It goes with the aglet thing. Anyone who knows sign will dismiss the word, and anyone who doesn't would dismiss the hitting of my fists together as nerves. If you think I'm in trouble, sign 'scared' with either one or two hands—with no expressions, of course."

"Any others?"

"Those are the main two. You sign better than I do. It isn't a very private language, so we've kept it to a minimum. You never know who can sign."

Andrew turned into the parking lot. "We can use it while I'm sweeping your room for bugs. I didn't find any cameras." *Yet.*

Miss Lee turned and smiled before unbuckling her seat belt. "You baited Stu and his people, didn't you?"

Andrew nodded. "I needed to know their response time. I'll also learn more about them when they are under stress."

Her smile grew. "I think I'm going to like working with you."

Andrew couldn't help but smile back even as his conscience yelled warnings about befriending clients.

PRINCESS PAWED AT THE WINDOW as Jordan waited for Andrew to get her door. He barely beat Stu to the handle. Jordan took a deep breath before facing them.

"You are supposed to notify us when you leave." Anger rolled off Stu.

Jordan set Princess on the ground and kept hold of the leash. "Stu, it's my day off. I'm at a dog park. The only way anyone will pay any attention to me is if Princess bites another dog—which she never does—or I cause a scene. Three big burly men marching around after me causes everyone to take notice. You guys have never followed me off set before."

"You haven't been shot at before." Stu crossed his arms.

Jordan took a breath to think of her next line as she slipped into the role her grandmother had played in a thriller movie from the fifties. Strong, confident, dismissive. "Then follow me if you must." She turned and headed for the high-fenced enclosure. Andrew fell in step next to her and left the other guards behind them.

Stu caught up and walked by her other side. "He doesn't need to be here."

"I hired Mr. Hastings, or Mr. Andrew, to protect Princess. We are at a dog park. There are mastiffs and poodles and other mutts. This is precisely where he needs to be." Jordan reached the double-gated entrance of the dog park and went through the gates Andrew held open. She turned to Stu. "I suggest if you are worried about my safety, you remain outside the gates. Inside, you will also have to worry about the safety of your shoes."

Once inside, she let Princess off the leash and moved to a bench under a tree, far from the exterior fence.

Andrew came to stand behind her. His energy differed from Blake's but was somehow still comforting. What made him tick?

Jordan played with the end of the leash. "Do you think I did the right thing with Stu?"

"Not my place to say, Miss Lee."

Jordan rolled her eyes. The gesture was big enough he should have seen it even from behind her back. "If I let him control me, I know it will be a very long six weeks. I don't want to fight him at every turn. And if you fight him, you'll be off the set. No offense, but I wish Blake were here."

"None taken. I'm sure he wishes he were here too. I have a ball for Princess. Would you like to throw it?"

Without a word, Jordan reached for the ball and lobbed it for her dog. How was she supposed to think with a handsome bodyguard standing so close?

Under the guise of taking a photo of the dog, Andrew took two of Stu and the bodyguard with him, neither of whom were doing a good job watching for dangers on their side of the chain-link fence. He sent the photos to Alan's account for his brother to check out on Monday morning. He needed to know if any of the guards among the Hearthfire crew were more or less than they appeared. The information Blake's wife had given him didn't include background checks on anyone with Hearthfire.

After September's experience with a less-than-competent body-guard, he knew he couldn't be too careful.

A text from Adam came through the secure Hastings app. **September asked around. Only Paul's movies and those on the main lot in California are excluding outside guards. Not unusual for the California lots. May not be a Hearthfire-wide policy.**

Andrew texted back. **Thanks. I found four bugs in her suite. At the moment, I'm assuming they're Hearthfire's. I don't think they have GPS. I will hide them in the dog park.**

—LOL. Should be entertaining.

The trick was placing them where a dog wouldn't find them and eat them. Andrew took the black bag Colin Ogilvie, one of their longtime clients, had designed to shield electronics like a portable Faraday cage. It was still in the testing phase, but it seemed to work. He walked around the large base of the nearest oak tree and removed the little listening devices from the bag. There were scratches in the tree's bark almost at his eye level. Perhaps the larger dogs chased squirrels up the trees. Andrew checked on Stu and the other guard before reaching as high up as he could and slipping two of the bugs into the V where a branch met the tree.

Then he walked to the interior fence separating one dog park section from another and placed the other two inside the poop-bag dispenser. He pulled out a bag in case Stu or his minion were watching.

He returned to the bench where Miss Lee threw the ball. Princess eyed it then sat down at Jordan's feet.

"Well, I guess she's done playing. Will you retrieve it for me?"

"Are you trying to teach me to fetch?" Andrew teased, hoping to see the real smile. When Miss Lee had exited the car, she'd become someone else. More guarded and stiff.

Jordan pulled her hair over her shoulder. "I don't think you would comply if that was my point." No smile came, but the harshness in her voice was gone. "I don't want to walk near the fence."

Andrew rescued the ball.

Stu glared through the fence. "Are you done yet?"

"That isn't my call," answered Andrew.

"Hurry her up, will you?"

Andrew looked around the park. "Have you found a threat?"

"No."

"If you find one, I'll get her out of here fast. She needs time with her dog." The principal's safety always came first. That included mental health, and this client needed dog time.

Stu frowned and walked away.

Andrew returned the ball to the backpack. Princess begged for a treat. He gave one of the tiny biscuits in the bag to Miss Lee.

Five minutes later, she stood. "I think we're done here."

When they reached the cars, Stu stopped them. "Miss Lee, if you will please come with us."

"I prefer to ride with Mr. Andrew."

"He's not your bodyguard."

Andrew stepped into the conversation. "Is that a standard rental car? It doesn't look like it's bulletproof."

"I don't know. The studio rented them."

"My vehicle is fully armored. I think the choice should be Miss Lee's." Andrew turned to Jordan.

"I think I'd rather be in the Hastings vehicle."

Andrew kept his bodyguard face as he assisted Miss Lee into the car under Stu's glare.

As Andrew drove the most direct route back to the hotel, Miss Lee relaxed. "Should you have taken him on?"

"We'll see. Your safety should be your choice—when you have one. Blake made it clear which of the two princesses I'm most responsible for. If I can offer you a safer option, I will. The choice is always yours."

"Thank you." Miss Lee stared out the window for the rest of the drive. Her perfume filled his car with a light, pleasant scent. One he shouldn't be noticing. "You call me Miss Lee. Just so you know, Blake's team calls me Jordan or Miss Jordan, and Grandma

Claire Lee. *Miss* and *missus* get confusing when we are together. Most of the time, the cast and crew call me Jordan too."

"Would you prefer I call you Jordan?"

"Yes, please. Do you mind if I call you Andrew? Since September always talks about you as Andrew, I think of you that way, without the mister in front."

"If that's what you're most comfortable with." Andrew debated the loss of formal names. Dad always said using formal names kept the client relationship in perspective. For now, he decided Miss Lee was safest.

At the hotel, to the obvious chagrin of Stu, Andrew accompanied Princess up to the third-floor suite. A florist box lay on the floor outside Jordan's door. Stu didn't halt the group, but the hair on the back of Andrew's neck bristled, and Princess growled low.

"Stop!" shouted Andrew. Stu and Jordan turned to face him. "That box outside Miss Lee's room shouldn't be there. Aren't you going to check it first?"

Stu muttered something before turning and continuing to the room. Jordan stayed next to Andrew. He handed Princess's leash to her and waved her back toward the elevator.

Stu picked up the long white box and opened it. A single black rose fell to the floor.

Andrew was blocking Jordan's view as Stu and the other bodyguard bent over the flower and the box.

"Let me see." Until now, she hadn't realized how big Andrew was. It was impossible to see over his shoulder or around him the way he was standing.

Andrew ignored her attempts to move him aside. "Stu, where is your secure room?"

"My room is two doors down."

She could see Andrew tense. "Your men are monitoring from two doors down and missed this?" Without waiting for an answer, Andrew spun around. "Miss Lee and Princess will be in 107 while you clear the area."

The Hastings bodyguard propelled them into the elevator so fast the door was closing before Stu could react and catch it.

And missed it.

Jordan hugged Princess tight enough the dog squirmed. "It was just a rose. I've gotten those before. It isn't a big deal." Saying a lie out loud didn't make it true.

"How many of those have been black?"

"One or two." Or a dozen? Blake didn't tell her everything.

"Did Blake let you near them?"

"Only photos."

"You shouldn't have seen this one either." Andrew stepped out of the elevator first, then ushered Jordan down the hall, where he tapped his keycard on the pad, letting them into a room.

Jordan stood near the door, unwilling to step any farther into a man's room. It was one of Grandma's rules: 'Never go into his hotel or bedroom.' Andrew didn't give her a choice. He steered her in and closed the door.

Andrew gave his room a quick check like Blake often did. "You should sit. Stu will be here any second."

A pounding on the door drowned out any other words Andrew had to say.

Jordan sat down in the chair closest to the window, holding Princess.

Andrew opened the door, and Stu pushed passed him. "What were you thinking? Why did you leave?"

Jordan refused to crane her neck to look up at him. Instead, she scratched Princess's ears and channeled her princess character. "I left because Andrew said to and you didn't say no."

"I was busy."

According to everything she'd learned and observed, that wasn't how bodyguards were supposed to work. Blake's team would have evacuated her as soon as they'd seen the box. Despite her curiosity, she knew the drill. "You know I wouldn't have seen the rose if Blake had been here. Someone put it here. Which means someone knows where I am."

Stu's lips formed a thin line. "The card wasn't addressed specifically to you. You don't know that."

Andrew butted into the conversation before Jordan could answer. "You have what? Eight, ten, bodyguards on your team? And Hearthfire rented out the entire third floor and half of the second. No one should have been able to leave anything for her."

Stu faced Andrew, hands clenched. "If you hadn't removed her from the building, there wouldn't have been a problem."

"Instead, they could have delivered the rose to her room with her in it."

"We were watching."

Andrew stepped well into Stu's personal space. "Like you did when we left the hotel? I shouldn't have gotten Miss Lee to the elevator and definitely not in my car before you responded. Where did you guys learn your trade? Online?"

What was Andrew doing? Trying to get her in trouble with the producer? Or get himself banned? Paul said he'd been willing to get another actress to take her place if she didn't sign the new contract, but she wasn't willing to let Princess Sam go to someone else. She'd worked hard to build the role, and with the new Princess Sam doll and the dress-clothesline, it was the first role she'd ever taken where merchandizing paid more than acting.

Stu leaned in. "I don't care if you are a Hastings—"

Jordan set Princess on the floor and stood, inserting herself between the men. "Hey, guys, let's not start a war here. I'm safe. Isn't that the point?"

Both men took a step back, though neither relaxed.

"Look, this weekend has everyone on edge, and Mr. Hastings is trying to figure out the whole guard-the-dog thing. Stu, if my room is clear, I'd like to take Princess up and have my dinner there."

Stu pulled out his phone and dialed. "Is it clear?" He waited a moment before hanging up. "Yes. You can bring the dog, but he stays here."

"Really?" Jordan raised an eyebrow like Grandma would and waited.

"He can come get the dog when you are done. I don't want him interfering again tonight."

Jordan picked up Princess's leash. "Fine, I'm starving." She followed Stu out of the room. She would have to worry about dealing with Andrew later. Obviously, Blake's men in California had not given him the entire picture.

Rod was leaving her room as she arrived. He whispered something to Stu. Stu turned to Jordan. "All clear, Miss Lee. I trust you won't leave again without informing me."

"Of course not. I order room service to which room?" Blake only allowed her to order to his room. Then he would move the food without inspecting it.

Stu paused as if the question had caught him off guard. "Mine."

Jordan locked the door after the Hearthfire guards left and did a quick scan of the room as Blake had taught her. Behind the lamp on the end table, she found a pea-sized device like the ones Andrew had located. Had he missed it before, or was it new?

Jordan sat down and invited Princess to join her on the couch. She held the dog close and whispered only loud enough for her to hear. "I'm scared."

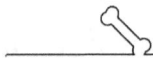

What on earth was Miss Lee thinking? Didn't she realize how inept the Hearthfire security team had shown themselves to be in the last two hours? Andrew glared at the door. She'd acted smart one minute, then all soft and incompetent the next. The key was that she'd *acted,* shifting personalities faster than a chameleon.

Andrew typed a quick report on his phone and sent it to Blake's people. He checked the time, wondering which of his brothers he could talk with, then sent out a text on the Hastings app, asking who was available.

Adam answered that he could call in two minutes.

Andrew used the time to order takeout. Tomorrow, he'd grab some groceries. The protein bars he kept in his go-bag only worked for so many meals before he'd starve rather than eat another.

Adam's call beeped in. "What's up?"

"Trying to decide if I should jump ship. The Hearthfire bodyguards are a disorganized mess. But then, when push comes to shove, Miss Lee sides with them over her own safety!"

"What happened?"

"I got her alone after finding the bugs in her suite. If there is a danger, either she doesn't know or doesn't want to talk about it. Kept changing the subject on me. Well, not exactly. She kept asking me personal questions. Then, it took HF nearly two blocks to catch up with us. We got out of the building with a dog and drove two blocks!" Unfathomable. No security team should allow that. "I'm one person. I can't protect her against whoever is out there and her guards' incompetence. All I can figure is they were watching the game and not the floor. Then, at the dog park, they spent the entire time watching either me or her."

"They must not have much experience or think you are her biggest threat."

Andrew paced the room. "We get back to her room and there's a white florist box leaning against her door. One bodyguard picks it up, and a black rose falls out. They've rented the entire floor. No one should have gotten near enough to her suite to deliver it. The front desk wouldn't have left it outside her door. The Hearthfire guards didn't even stop her from getting close. I did."

"Can you imagine how fast Dad would fire them?"

"I'm thinking they're actors. 'I'm not really a bodyguard, but I've played one on TV.'" Andrew deepened his voice, mocking the "bodyguards."

Adam laughed. "Imagine a *Real Bodyguards* TV show about standing around all day hoping nothing happens."

"Back to what happened. The HF bodyguards stand there staring at the rose, I bring her down to my room since they don't have a secure place. Ten minutes later Stu gets up in my face about it, and she defends him. Then she leaves with him and goes back to her room. I can't be on call 24/7 and protect her from her bodyguards plus whoever is threatening her. Not to mention care for her dog. This won't work. If she won't take her own safety seriously, what am I supposed to do?"

Guarding a celeb was never a one-person job. And guarding one who'd been shot at? Andrew needed a team. Jordan would be better off with no personal bodyguard so she didn't have a false sense of security. But Hastings had never failed a client. This job could well be the first where something happened to their principal, and Andrew wasn't willing to take that chance.

"How do you know she isn't taking her security seriously?"

"Too many personal questions? I get Mr. Blake's been her body-guard for over twenty years and she is stressed, but this is not the time to get chummy with the bodyguards." Andrew didn't point out how much easier it would be if she were rude or snooty.

Adam paused before responding. "Are you quitting?"

"Hastings don't quit." And that was the dilemma—stay and face the disgrace of failure or leave and be a quitter.

"Um, sometimes we do." Adam's voice was slightly strangled. Andrew winced. Adam had quit a job, and it had turned out disastrous for everyone involved.

"Sorry, wasn't thinking."

"There are jobs we don't take. Sometimes a client isn't a good fit. This job has unusual constraints. Blake has been with Jordan for over two decades. Even with our longest-term clients, we've switched team leaders. Jordan probably doesn't understand what she needs to tell you."

"Was September clueless about her safety?"

"To a point. She remembers when Dad used to be the body-guard on her parents' tours and Mom being on the set. There were years September's family used other firms because Hast-ings wasn't big enough to do the national or international thing then. Bodyguards are a natural part of her life. I don't know that September could tell me what we do all day for her."

"Then why doesn't Blake have someone from his own crew come out here?"

"No clue. You said he was in a lot of pain last night. Did you get to talk to him today?"

Andrew sat on the edge of one of the upholstered chairs—not half as comfortable as it looked. "No. I dealt with the dog. The call I made to Blake's office was somewhat helpful. His wife is the office manager. They run a lean team, with only enough manpower for Miss Lee and her grandmother Claire Lee. Shouldn't Mr. Blake have a backup plan in place?"

"Maybe? But that isn't the point. Jordan called September, and Mr. Blake approved of using Hastings Security. Right now, we are the backup plan."

Andrew remembered how Blake's face relaxed when Andrew confirmed he was one of Jethro's sons. "Which takes me back to how bad it would look if I quit."

"Think on it tonight. You can talk to Mr. Blake tomorrow. From what you said last night, the briefing was bare bones. Maybe there's something more he can fill you in on when he isn't suffering the immediate aftereffects of surgery."

"True. Anything more on yesterday's shooting?"

"No, the videos we found are down now. I guess the police don't want them going viral. Alan might know more tomorrow."

"I don't like this. It feels like I'm in a movie where the audience is screaming at me not to turn the next corner but I follow the cute girl anyway."

"If I were you, I'd wait another day and get more facts. Quitting in haste is not a good idea."

Someone tapped at Andrew's door. Dinner. "Thanks, bro."

"Anytime."

Andrew hit the end button and answered the door. He tipped the delivery driver extra for being quick.

An hour later, he got a text from Miss Lee. **Come get Princess.**

Andrew took the stairs to work out his annoyance at being a glorified dog walker.

A Hearthfire bodyguard leaned back in a chair outside Miss Lee's room, playing on his phone. He didn't look up until Andrew was three feet away. Then he stood. "What do you need?"

"Miss Lee messaged me about the dog."

"Fine, go in."

Andrew knocked, and Jordan opened the door wide. "Come on in."

As soon as Miss Lee shut the door, she held up another bug. "Princess is on the balcony."

Andrew followed her to the balcony, then she signed, "Don't make Stu upset. I don't want you kicked off the set."

He knelt down next to Princess and scratched her ears. "Where was the bug?"

"Is it safe to talk out here?" whispered Miss Lee.

"I have a signal blocker. Only works about a ten-foot radius, though."

"On the lamp next to the couch."

Andrew frowned. "There wasn't one there earlier. I can keep removing them, or we can ignore them."

"At least we can sign. If it is Stu's bug, we will only make him upset, which will make Paul upset with me."

"You didn't tell Stu?"

"Blake may respect him but he doesn't like him for a reason. I don't need to know the reason to be wary. So he isn't the first person I'll trust." Miss Lee rolled her eyes. "I'm not stupid."

"I didn't say you were. Anything you have to tell me? I'll wear out my welcome in another minute."

Miss Lee studied the tree line. "Thanks for doing your job." A small smile lit her face, and she walked back into the suite, Princess following her.

Maybe she was more aware of her safety than he thought. Miss Lee wasn't the first actor Hastings had worked for who'd been hard to read. Alex would be better suited to this client, but with his new bride and baby, he wouldn't take the job. Andrew couldn't walk away.

"Where's the leash?"

"I know I set it—" Miss Lee turned in a slow circle.

Andrew spotted it under the coffee table. Princess jumped, her excited dancing momentarily blocking his view as he reached for it, connecting with Jordan's hand instead of the leash.

Jordan's wide eyes met his over the coffee table. Andrew let go of her hand but not the sensation left by the touch.

Jordan set the leash on the table, her face a shade pinker. Andrew studied the hand he'd just held. Her fingers were long and slender, something he'd noted as she signed, but his awareness had nothing to do with the shape of her hand. It was the way her hand fit in his. Jordan's eyes were still on him, her mouth a silent O. Princess looked from her master to Andrew before leaping to Jordan's side.

No way. This was not happening. Attraction to the client was a huge no-go area for him. His reaction to touching her must have been a fluke—it was just surprise at finding her hand and not the cold plastic of the leash handle.

Someone tapped on the door, and Andrew snapped the leash onto Princess's collar. "Do you want her back tonight?"

Jordan blinked twice before answering. "Um, no. I think I need sleep, and in a new place, she gets up in the night. Then I have to wake up half the building because I can't take her outside myself."

Again, Miss Lee was showing a sense of self-preservation. Andrew took the end of Princess's leash. "Good night, then."

Miss Lee opened the door to let him out. Stu stood there with his fist up, preparing to knock. "You didn't need to take so long."

"Sorry, Stu, it was my fault. I misplaced the leash. Good night, Princess. Be a good girl." She looked at Andrew, her face unreadable.

Andrew nodded and turned, but not before he caught a flash of something that looked like an ILY sign. Was that for him or the dog? He should quit before he became a victim of the family curse. If only he could be sure she would be safe.

THE THEME FROM A FIFTY'S musical woke Jordan at 5:00 a.m. She rubbed her eyes before answering. "Good morning, Grandma."

"It sounds like I woke you up. Did I do my math wrong?"

"I don't know. Did you intend to wake me up at 5:00 a.m. on Monday?"

"Good thing you are aren't in LA. Sorry, bunny. I wanted to talk with you after yesterday's texts and phone messages. How are you?"

"I'm fine. The bodyguard I hired for Princess is taking good care of me. From the look on his face last night when I chose to listen to Stu over him, I thought he might quit, but maybe not. I don't know how to explain all the politics behind everything and I am afraid that Paul will refuse me even one bodyguard. Mr. Andrew is harder to read than Blake." Which was wonderful and scary but in a different way.

"I spoke with Blake yesterday. He seemed to think this Hastings kid—his words not mine—would do a very good job. Blake was initially concerned about his age but hopes it won't be an issue."

"Andrew is very competent." As soon as she said his name she knew she slipped.

"First-name basis?"

"There are five brothers and a father, all Mr. Hastings. Andrew normally goes by Mr. Andrew. September Platt never uses *mister*, so I guess I think of him by his first name."

"Oh." A long pause filled the space, and Jordan checked the connection.

Grandma's voice came back on. "Blake said Andrew is good-looking."

Had Blake noticed her attraction to the youngest Hasting? She had been on painkillers, and Blake needed to be. It was just a fluke. Like the leash. "He has some nice features."

"Is this going to be a problem?"

"You mean the knight-in-shining-armor thing? Falling for my rescuer? Not particularly, since I'm not falling for him." Leaning a slight bit, but not falling.

"Jordan, you know what I mean. It's like what happened with that leading man—your first semi-real kiss. Knowing it could happen and it would be fake didn't stop a crush from happening." Again with her first leading-man crush a decade ago. Yes, she thought she'd fallen for him and even dated him for a while, but he'd wanted to be seen with her more than be with her. Jordan had learned her lesson. Grandma didn't need to bring it up again.

"Andrew would make a great medieval knight. He has the looks and the compassion. But I'm not a damsel in distress. And it's been years since I mistook an on-screen kiss as anything other than acting."

The pause on the other end was longer than needed for an overseas call. "I fly to London today and will finish up by Friday. I've been wondering if I should change my plans and come straight to Wisconsin rather than LA."

"Keep to your plans. Coming out here won't do anything helpful at the moment. Paul doesn't need any more surprises. You know how he is."

"It would be a personal visit."

"Paul wouldn't see it that way." Jordan didn't want to disrupt Grandma's schedule.

"You're right. Paul doesn't handle external stress well, does he?"

"Not if he thinks it could affect his career, and you visiting me after this week's mess could mean you have no faith in him."

"Because I don't."

Jordan laughed.

"It isn't funny. You should have an entire team out there, not just Blake."

"I know, Grandma. I'm glad Blake was here. September says the Hastings are the best, although she may be biased. I'll be fine."

"I'll let you get back to sleep now. Sorry about my math skills. I'll try to call later next time."

"Love you, Grandma."

"Love you too, bunny. Remember what I said about knights in shining armor." The call disconnected, and Jordan checked the time. Another hour of sleep or annoy the bodyguard and go run on the treadmill? The latter would only be fun if it was Andrew. She mentally replayed the moment they'd both dived for the leash. It was only a moment. Like the ones in dozens of scripts. Those didn't happen in real life, did they?

There was no rule saying the princess and the knight had to get together. They could be friends, right? Jordan closed her eyes and replayed last night. In a movie script, it would have been the moment where the audience raised their eyebrows and said, "I told you they would be a couple." It was odd not to have a director yell "Cut!" to end it. These moments didn't happen in real life. And if they did, they couldn't mean anything. Maybe Grandma was right, Andrew was just a very convenient knight in shining armor.

Jordan's kiss was cold and wet on Andrew's cheek. Not the way this moment should end. Andrew turned his head to refocus the kiss, and Jordan whimpered like a dog.

Andrew opened his eyes. Princess whimpered again, her chin

resting on his chest. He sat up, relieved he hadn't carried his dream kiss to fruition. A dream about a client? A first he didn't want to repeat. Andrew pushed the covers back. "Do you need to go outside, girl?"

By the time he got back to his room last night, he knew he wasn't going to quit the job. And the decision had nothing to do with the momentary awareness he had of his client. Calling her Miss Lee helped him keep his distance, though he'd slipped a few times because of their meeting in the hospital. He'd need to make sure he only thought and talked and dreamed of Jordan as Miss Lee. She was off-limits.

Yellows and golds tinted the eastern sky. Andrew stretched while Princess inspected the lawn. The dream, though it had faded, hadn't left his mind. He'd never dreamed about a client before. How could he protect a client if he wasn't objective? A dog jumping on his bed should have woken him up. Was his subconscious trying to tell him to quit the job or to stay?

His phone pinged. Andrew checked the app. It was Adam.

Just checking in.

Nothing new, but the day is young. I wish I had a backup here, preferably female.

—Tonie is available. What if I bring her up tomorrow, with September, more as an undercover thing? We could leave her with Jordan at night.

Could you be vaguer with that plan?

—I'll try. I need to see if Mom can help me brainstorm cover ideas.

Firms all over the country contracted Melanie Hastings for her covert planning skills. Andrew reread the words. What he needed was advice. But the Hastings app, though secure, wasn't necessarily private.

Call?

The phone rang. "I'm driving to the office gym to meet Alex. What's up?"

"How did you stay professional around September when you

58

first realized you were attracted to her?"

"A load of denial, which made it worse in the end. Why?"

"Just wondering."

"Did something happen with Jordan?"

"Not really. I dreamed about her. I've never dreamed about a client the way I dreamed about her." This was way too embarrassing. Why had he asked for a call?

"Good thing too. I can't imagine what Colin Ogilvie would do to you if you admitted you'd dreamed about his wife the way you are implying." Since Colin could hack into anything in the world, the possibilities were endless. Andrew had been handling for Candice Ogilvie since Colin married her as his primary account. Protecting Colin was easy, he only left his computer when his wife made him. Mrs. Ogilvie was another matter, she'd randomly detour to a children's hospital, or neglect to tell them about a speaking appointment. When he dreamed of Mrs. Ogilvie it was usually a nightmare involving paparazzi disguised as sick children and everyone had rainbow hair.

Andrew followed the dog back inside. "Ha-ha. I think it must be because this job has me worried about things. It might help if the Hearthfire guards were better trained. The whole guarding her against unknown threats and the guards' incompetence has me overanalyzing everything."

"So, are you over analyzing enough to dream-kiss your client?"

"We didn't kiss ..."

"I knew it. What happened?" Suppressed laughter laced Adam's voice.

"Last night, I went up to get the dog. Miss Lee found another bug. She warned me about fighting with Stu, and I realized that she was playing things smart when it came to the guards and was aware of her safety. I saw the real her for a few unguarded moments, and we connected. Stupid, right? Nothing happened." That was as close to explaining the simple touch as he would get.

"Did you want it to?"

"No way!" Andrew lowered his voice. "I will not follow the family curse. Forget I said anything about it."

"Curse?"

"You know, breaking the client/guard barrier. It's one of the cardinal rules of being a bodyguard: don't get too personal with the client. Marriage is way too personal. Our family is getting a reputation."

"Two days and you are thinking marriage?"

"No! I'm talking you and September, Abbie and Preston, Alex and Kimberly, not to mention whatever is or is not happening with Alan and Elle. Deidre says our firm has a reputation."

Adam laughed. "Maybe, but have you ever seen your siblings happier? Look, Andrew, I know how much you hate following in our footsteps, but when it comes to love, follow your heart. Don't be so caught up in not following us or following the rules you don't let it happen. I was lucky I got a second chance. And it isn't like we followed a pattern. Alex married Kimberly when they only knew each other a day."

So not helping. Andrew searched for the words to end the conversation.

Adam spoke again. "As far as your nothing-happened thing. It could be a trust moment. You've had those with clients before. And if ever you had a client you needed to trust you, it's Jordan Lee."

"That makes sense, and after the rose incident, I needed to trust her. Will you talk to Mom and Tonie? I do need a second set of eyes up here."

"Will do."

Andrew ended the call, glad he'd found a reasonable excuse for the irrational thoughts he had.

His phone pinged, and Jordan's icon popped up.

—Paul arranged for a spa day to "calm my nerves." Dog park later? Yes.

He scratched Princess's ears. "Looks like it's just you and me, girl."

The dog's eyes grew large, and she tilted her head. Perhaps she was as disappointed as he was.

"Imagine. Two more months and I can paint my nails whatever color I want." Reggie, who played Princess Sam's sidekick, put the bottle of bright-orange nail polish back on the shelf and chose a neutral shade.

Jordan picked up a bottle of clear polish. "Not for long. You'll have another role locked up soon."

"When I do, it won't have as many restrictions as Hearthfire's. And I'll get to wear whatever dress I want when I walk the red carpet."

A gasp interrupted Reggie's comment, and they turned to see Kittie, one of the crew members, duck her head.

"Kittie, I'm not shaming the Hearthfire name. I'm just tired of living a PG-rated life on and off screen. Haven't you ever wanted a bit of scandal in your life?"

"Nope. When I get my big break, I don't want people pulling up old web pages claiming I only got there because I was a media hound." Kittie tugged on her ponytail.

The head makeup artist, Maria, frowned but didn't say anything as she picked a sparkly purple polish.

Suzi, the actress who played the forty-year-old maid, patted Kittie on the back. "You'll get your break one of these days. I appreciate what you do for us around the set." They wandered off in the direction of the foot baths.

"Why did Paul send Kittie here with us? To be his little spy?" Reggie whispered.

"She works as hard as the rest of us." Jordan wondered how much longer the day could go on.

Reggie walked away, leaving Jordan alone with Maria.

"This isn't helping, is it? How are you doing?" The stylist picked up one bottle after another.

Jordan placed a bottle of peach polish back on the shelf. "I still have a mild headache, and no, a spa day is not helping. Will you be able to cover my new scar?"

Maria put her hand to her heart and rolled her eyes. "I should be insulted that you even ask. Remember the road rash from your skateboarding accident when you were thirteen? This is simple compared to that."

"You know I love you for more than your magic makeup wands, right?"

"I do. And I would like to point out that you don't even need to stay if the result is going to be more of a headache."

Before Jordan could answer, a worker in black scrubs approached. "Miss Lee? Your masseuse is ready for you. If you will come this way."

Jordan followed the employee to the back rooms of the spa.

The dim lights and scented candles did little to calm Jordan. She asked for only a neck and shoulder massage so she could keep her shirt on. Having strangers touch her was not something she enjoyed. How Paul thought this would be relaxing was beyond her. The unanswered questions about the shooting were worse than any conversation about nail color. Only Maria had asked Jordan how she was doing. The makeup artist was the only member of the group Jordan spoke to outside of work. She used to hang around with Reggie, but they'd grown apart this last year as they'd auditioned for the same roles and Reggie spent more time at parties than at work.

When the pan-pipe music ended, the massage therapist indicated Jordan could leave.

Alone in the dressing room, Jordan texted Andrew. **I need to visit Blake. Not sure how to make it happen. Will you find a way to meet me?**

—Yes, I was about to go see him. Will Princess be all right alone?

Do you have her crate?

—Yes.

Make sure she has water and a large bone. She'll be good for three hours.

—Let me know what time, and I'll be in his room waiting.

Jordan made a call to Stu, who grumbled but agreed. She texted Andrew with the time, then moved on to getting her hands dipped in warm wax.

As predicted, the doctors had moved Mr. Blake to another room. Andrew tapped on the door before entering.

"Come in, Mr. Hastings, although I assume you go by Mr. Albert, or Abner, or whatever *A* name is yours. I apologize for not remembering."

"It's Andrew, and no apologies needed. My mother always had to run through the entire bag of *A* names before finding me too. You look like you're feeling better."

"I am. They will let me out in the morning. They would have this morning, except the doctor didn't want me flying. He still doesn't. I've always wanted to cross the country by train, and this will be my chance."

"You're going alone?"

"No, my wife flew in last night. She's the one you spoke to on the phone."

"I'm happy she could come out. She didn't mention it on the phone. I would have expected her not to be so composed with you having been shot. It took me a moment to realize I was speaking with your wife."

"She is amazing, isn't she? My brother and I run our tiny firm together. We only have Jordan and Claire Lee as clients. Mostly, we hire temps for big jobs and have a core of six guards. One is on his honeymoon, and the rest are in India. I didn't think it through when I asked you to call." Blake shook his head.

"Considering you were less than an hour post-op, you did a great job of passing on information." Andrew pulled the chair into a position where he could comfortably see the door and talk to Mr. Blake. "I don't think I would have been half as focused."

"You got the link to the app I sent you, right?"

"Yes. The same company that made ours made it. Jordan also gave me her panic word. We are working on our communication."

"On set, she can't have her phone with her and probably not in the readings either. So you've got to pay attention to her signs. She's only used her word twice on set when it wasn't in the script. Both times, a costar made her uncomfortable. She'll tell you if *aglet* is in the script." Mr. Blake pushed another pillow under his elbow to support his arm.

Andrew decided the bodyguard was coherent enough to answer his questions. "Have you seen any footage from the shooting Saturday?"

"Only what the police detective showed me."

Andrew pulled out his phone. "These clips were up on one of the social media channels. We snagged copies of them before they got taken down."

Blake watched the three clips. "The police showed me the second one. And one similar to the first." He played the third one again, pausing and rewinding.

The last clip had been posted on a less-popular website by an anonymous cell-phone user who'd panned the audience seconds before the shooting began. The man identified by the police as the shooter stood five feet from one of the Hearth-fire bodyguards. The camera passed the bodyguard, then the picture jumped, capturing a ducking crowd and then the pavement at the sound of the first shot. Three more gunshots could be heard distinctly, with a pause before the last. The next part of the video showed the bodyguard wrestling with the shooter.

Andrew took his phone back. "It's the third video that concerns us. The shooter got off four shots, taking time to adjust his aim before the guard only five feet away reacted. Unfortunately, this doesn't show the shooter in the act."

"Has Jordan seen this?"

"I haven't shown her, and she said she was avoiding watching media on Saturday, so my guess is no."

"That last clip you have makes it seem like the shooter wanted to hit me. The police didn't ask any questions to indicate they thought I might be the target."

"Has there been a threat that might have been aimed at you?" The question had to be asked, even if Andrew didn't like the ramifications.

"No, just the usual. Jordan's biggest problems are the so-claimed psychics or real-life psychos who claim to know where her parents are living, buried, or hiding. She has a fairly persistent fan who proposes by email on the fourth day of every month. At first we thought he'd escalated to the black roses and notes found on the set over the last six months, but he says no."

"You know who he is?"

"The fourth-of-the-month proposal guy? Yes. He's never threatened her and doesn't come to any events. There isn't a law against proposing. There are two standing restraining orders on former stalkers, but both men are currently incarcerated on unrelated charges. The new activity doesn't link with the old stuff. This is the longest she's had a stalker we couldn't trace. It doesn't help that some things happen at the studio and I can't always see the evidence. Stu isn't great about sharing."

"Someone delivered a black rose to her room last night. I didn't get a good look at it. I don't like how the Hearthfire guards dealt with the unexpected gift."

"I can guess. You got Jordan out of there?" asked Blake.

"Not fast enough. I didn't realize the Hearthfire guards weren't going to. I don't like the hotel arrangement. A private rental would be easier to guard."

"Ditto. The show has done five other location shoots over the years, and I've always rented a house. This is the first time they've insisted on everyone staying together. Coupled with the fact that Hearthfire recently denied Jordan her own bodyguards, it makes me think most of the odd things this past month are coming from within. If I was the target, someone is playing a long game and knows I was the only one protecting Jordan."

Andrew tapped his chin. There had to be more. "Can you tell me more about her contract? Jordan was rather vague."

"This end-of-the-series special wasn't in the original contract. Hearthfire has financial issues, and they're cutting some of their series shows. This one was slated to be dropped at the end of last season, but the fans like it so much they chose to do a half season with a grand finale. This meant they had to find someone to take the princess off to her happily ever after, a Prince Charming. Storm Tordon is a huge coup for them. After they signed him, they distributed the new contracts. I wasn't surprised they were keeping bodyguards off set. That's pretty standard for closed sets. Actors with active threats can usually keep one nearby. But this location shoot"—Blake shook his head—"only the continuing actors have the restrictions. Storm and his entourage are not staying on-site. Claire Lee will have her own accommodations for the three or four days they'll film her piece. As you may know, the singer September will have her own guards. If Claire Lee hadn't stepped in, I wouldn't have been here. No one in management thinks for a moment that I'm truly guarding the dog. But the concession worked on paper. I can be anyplace Jordan wants the dog. I asked Donetta to renegotiate after the shooting. No go."

Not much new in the telling. But if Hearthfire was having money issues, it seemed they would prefer to use personal security so they could save money. "They are trying to keep me out of her rooms. So far, we've found six listening devices."

"Six? I've never found over two. They are most likely Stu's. As far as keeping you out of her suite, you're young and handsome. They could use that against you—Jordan's squeaky-clean reputation and all. I don't think they've ever had to give her a warning about her conduct. An older bodyguard like your father wouldn't raise the same concerns or, better yet, your mother. But I understand they don't work out of the office often."

"If Hearthfire is worried about reputation, why hire Storm? He isn't exactly discreet about his love life. And it's not squeaky clean." Even Andrew had seen the articles and he usually avoided gossip media.

Mr. Blake shrugged. The answer was evident. Storm Tordon's popularity was unrivaled.

"I was thinking of trying to bring one of our female guards on." *And quitting this job.* Since he was staying, there was no point in telling Blake about his doubts.

Blake scratched his stubbly chin. "I don't know how Stu would react to that. She might end up with less access than you have."

"But they couldn't keep her out of Jordan's suite."

"True. I wonder if there's a way I can keep you on too. If the stalker is someone on the crew, they might not see a female bodyguard as the same protection."

"All our female guards are as capable as our men."

Blake laughed so hard he had to reach up and hold his shoulder. "Don't get defensive. I fully appreciate the skills of a good female guard. The best part is that most of them don't look the part, which always gives them an advantage."

"Any way we could bring someone in undercover? I don't know enough about the movie industry."

"Claire has a specific hairdresser and makeup artist. Unfortunately, that's not the case for Jordan. Maria is a Hearthfire employee." Mr. Blake furrowed his brow. "You could get a dog groomer or specialist. Have Jordan claim the shooting stressed Princess out and the dog needs special care. Paul will balk but give in, and the job doesn't cross over yours. Since he isn't paying the bill, it might work."

"I like that. And it would give her a reason to stay in the suite with Jordan. I'll call the office and have them see if any of our female bodyguards have a background with dogs. What else do I need to know about Jordan's threat file?"

"I'll send it over as soon as I can get to my laptop. But I'd watch my back if I were you. If someone wanted me out of the picture, you're next."

Not good. A bodyguard who was a target could just as well endanger their principal as help them.

Stu left Rod in the sitting area a few doors down from Blake's room and approached Jordan. "I'll walk you to the door. I have a good line of sight from here, and hospitals get rather annoyed at people standing around in the hallway."

Who knew HIPAA could be useful for getting rid of unwanted bodyguards? Jordan knocked once and opened the door. She waited until Stu retreated before fully entering the room and closing the door. "How are you feeling?" She crossed the room to Blake's side.

Andrew vacated the chair next to the bed. "Would you like me to leave?"

"Not yet. Stu is watching the room, and it's probably best if he doesn't know you're here." Jordan took the offered chair and proceeded to ask Blake a litany of questions regarding his health and recovery. Andrew stood near the window, giving them as much privacy as possible in the small room.

Satisfied with Blake's answers, Jordan turned to Andrew. "I want to know both your opinions. Should I be concerned over Hearthfire's lack of security since the shooting? It should have ramped up, not gotten worse."

Andrew and Blake did the guy thing where they looked at each other and measured what they would say.

Blake took the lead. "I've made no secret of how I feel about Stu and his team. Andrew told me about last night. If Hearthfire isn't going to watch out for you, you need to be more careful. If you see another box or note, leave, even if you have to drag a bodyguard with you. If they are compromising your safety because they don't have the budget, why limit your personal security team if we aren't on their payroll?"

"Blake, we've been over it a thousand times. It doesn't make sense. But after last night, you can bet I'll be more careful. I knew I should have left, but you can't blame me for being curious."

Andrew stepped closer to the bed. "One of my biggest concerns is there is only one of me. I think I have a solution, but it will require some acting on your part."

Jordan batted her eyes. "Didn't you hear? That's what I do best."

Andrew's jaw tightened as he tried to hide a smile. He explained bringing in a Hastings Security employee as a specialized doggy caretaker.

"I can work with that. Paul sent me to the silly spa today mostly to make sure I was calm and prepared. I think he's afraid I'll lose it. Near hysterics over my poor Princess, I can hire any dog whisperer I want."

Blake laughed. "A spa day? Paul doesn't know you well, does he? He could have saved money and sent you to the local bookstore."

"If they have good seating, I can spend all day there." She suppressed a sigh. A bookstore would be heaven right now. There were two new releases she was dying to get her hands on. "I haven't been on a good book binge for a couple months. The shooting schedule has been crazy this summer."

Andrew came to stand at the foot of Blake's bed. "September asked around, and this production seems to be the only one limiting personal security. Why?"

Jordan looked at Blake before she spoke. "My theory is Storm. Everything changed when he signed on. He let Paul know he was very annoyed when I wouldn't go out with him."

Blake nodded his agreement. "We've hashed this out dozens of times, and it all comes back to Storm. The only thing is, he's been in New Zealand shooting his next big blockbuster for the last three months, so the notes and things left around the set don't point to him. And stalkers rarely use assistants to do their work."

"Someone could exploit the lack of security." Andrew crossed his arms. To Jordan, he looked like he was ready to take on the world in his own action movie. He would make a decent leading man. Handsome but not unbelievably so. Good muscles, nice eyes. *Nope, nope, nope. Not going there.*

Blake cleared his throat. Had she been staring? She pretended to check her phone.

"It would have been easy for a cast or crew member to get the rose to Jordan's room, and it would mean Stu's team isn't as lax as we think." Blake took a sip of water from a huge hospital mug.

"Someone on the floor would have needed only seconds to put the box in front of the door. They could have placed it while we were on the elevator, assuming Stu received an all clear."

Jordan thought of her costars, who were also staying on that floor. "I've worked with most of these actors for three years. Why would they want to hurt or scare me?"

Blake shook his head. "People are odd creatures prone to stupidity."

Andrew smiled.

Oh, wow, she liked that smile complete with a dimple. Jordan tried to focus on something else. She didn't need someone sabotaging her if her hormones would do that for her. Who'd given them a script and forgotten to tell her about it?

Her phone pinged. "That's Stu. I guess I better go." Jordan stood and leaned over Blake, giving him a kiss on the cheek. She turned and sidestepped to miss hitting the chair. Instead, she fell into Andrew. She caught herself with a hand on his chest. Oh yes, he had muscles.

He steadied her, placing a gentle yet strong hand on her waist. Jordan looked up at his blue eyes. The little flecks in them reminded her of the ocean after a storm. Part of her waited for someone to yell "Cut!" She couldn't remember what she should say, his nearness having stolen her every thought. "Sorry?"

Andrew dropped his hand. "My fault. I was trying to get to the chair."

Jordan nodded and checked her phone, hoping any blush would pass. "I'll ask Stu to stop at a bookstore. That should give you time to get back to the hotel. Princess will need a walk."

Jordan slipped out of the room before she could say anything stupid. Sorry with a question mark? That was lame. She hadn't meant to put the blame on him. Maybe it was best if he thought she wasn't so bright. But if he had any romantic thoughts like hers, she wasn't sorry at all.

Andrew returned the chair to its proper place, keeping his back to Mr. Blake. He needed to be professional, even if his racing heart wasn't. "Do you need anything before I go?"

Mr. Blake studied Andrew for what felt like hours. "No, I don't think so. I've been the closest thing to a father my girl has had since she was eight. I'm trying to decide if I need to give you a fatherly lecture or not."

"My father gives me plenty of those, sir. As the youngest, I get them every time he has to give them to an older sibling."

"According to rumor, he's given a few lectures about getting involved with clients and they haven't all worked." Mr. Blake frowned.

Andrew shifted his weight. Mr. Blake's accusations weren't completely true. Alex had never gotten a lecture partially because he'd fake-married his wife to protect her, then realized that there wasn't much fake about it. Abbie had gotten a lecture, but she was undercover as a fiancée. Adam had received all the standard lectures and, well, those may have backfired a bit. "I see your point, sir."

"Maybe, maybe not. Remember, if you act on whatever happened between you two just now, I'm watching, and I will take a bullet for my girl. So if you aren't willing to stand between me and a bullet, then stay out of the way."

"Yes, sir."

"Good. I think we understand each other. Now, go keep my girl safe."

Andrew drove away from the hospital knowing he wouldn't abandon the job, yet he still wasn't sure when he'd come to that conclusion. It could have been when he grabbed Jordan's hand instead of the leash, although her hand placed over his rapidly beating heart had sealed the deal. Nothing would happen to her. He needed another bodyguard up here sooner than later. Preferably before Dad had a reason to give him a lecture about falling for a client.

Jordan inspected the bags under her eyes in the mirror. Nightmares had punctuated last night's sleep. If Princess had been allowed to stay the night, she might have slept better. However, after the confrontation with Stu and Paul when Andrew had come to take Princess out for her evening bathroom break, it wasn't worth the trouble. Paul and Stu had refused to let Andrew past the doorframe. They placed some other bodyguard in the hall that Princess hated. Which led to enough barking that someone called the front desk, who called Paul. Good thing they were not shooting today. Maria would have had an exceptionally difficult time with Jordan's makeup, even without having to deal with the healing cut on her head.

The read-through started at ten. Perhaps she could talk Stu into another trip to the dog park before then. She needed to tell Andrew about the bug she found last night in the smaller bedroom. She wanted Blake's advice about dealing with her new personal security, but she couldn't call him when she knew someone had bugged her suite. If the listening devices belonged to Hearthfire, they might be in breach of her contract, which could give her the leverage to renegotiate her contract. If they hadn't placed them, maybe someone was waiting for her to rehearse her lines, although that would be pointless since the script so closely followed the book series anyway. Or it could be some overeager paparazzi. Either way, she couldn't keep ignoring their existence.

She should go work out. Too bad swimming was out this week. The doctor had told her to keep her head as dry as possible and to have someone help her wash her hair when needed. Dry shampoo would suffice for today if she didn't do a sweaty workout. So stretches it was.

A quick shower and a bowl of oatmeal later, Jordan texted Andrew. **If I can get Paul and Stu to agree, dog park at 8:30?**

—She's been on a jog.

Come on, read between the lines! Jordan didn't know if willing him to understand would work or not. **I'd love to see her.**

—I'm sure she would like to see you too. Let me know if they agree. Will do.

Jordan walked across the hall and tapped on Stu's door, amazed that they weren't watching her more closely. A new bodyguard answered. How annoying. If they kept changing guards, how was she supposed to know who she could trust? The Burgundy polo with the Hearthfire logo wasn't all that different from some of the ones sold online. "I'm taking Princess to the park at eight thirty. I assume someone will accompany me?"

Rod appeared behind the new guard. "I'll arrange it, Miss Lee. Stu is in a meeting."

"Thanks. I'll see you in fifteen minutes."

The bodyguards closed the door. She was back across the hall and opening her own door when the door to Stu's room flew open and Stu ran from the room. "Miss Lee, what were you doing in the hallway?"

"Arranging for an escort to the dog park."

"You could have called."

"I suppose I could have." Jordan retreated into her room, closing the door. Blake would have freaked out if she had been able to leave her room unnoticed when he had been in charge. Andrew might too. Should she tell him? She sent a quick text to Andrew confirming the eight-thirty dog-park walk.

Stu and one other guard met her when she answered her door at 8:29. The walk down the hall to the elevator would have been good practice for someone playing the role of a death-row inmate.

Andrew and Princess waited outside next to a new SUV. "I see you upgraded your rental, Stu."

Stu opened the back-passenger door of the SUV. Andrew didn't point out that his car was still better.

Jordan had little choice but to enter the SUV or cause a scene like her dog was, jumping and dancing and tangling her leash around them. "One minute. If I don't say hello to Princess, she will be impossible to handle."

Trying to keep the dog hair to a minimum, Jordan crouched down. "Good morning, girl. How are you? Have you been good? Did last night turn out differently than you expected?" She looked up at Andrew, hoping he'd realize the question was for him more than the dog.

Princess took advantage of Jordan's distraction to land a sloppy dog kiss on her neck.

"Yes, I missed you too. Yes, I know we need to work things out." Jordan scratched behind Princess's ears and stood. "I'll see you at the dog park."

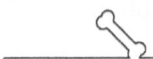

Andrew put Princess in her car seat, a contraption rivaling his nephews' car seats for difficulty of use. Thankfully, Princess sat patiently, allowing him to connect the straps and safety vest. The SUV Jordan was riding in left the lot. Since Paul had refused to allow Jordan to leave the hotel last night, he hoped they would get some time to talk at the dog park.

Andrew checked his Hastings app and the one Blake had provided before leaving the parking lot. The SUV headed for the same park they'd used Sunday. Alan would probably yell at Andrew for tagging a vehicle not belonging to a client. At the moment, Andrew felt no guilt. He needed every advantage he could get. At this point, he would tag Stu and Paul if he could find a way to keep them from noticing.

Stu waited with Jordan at the gate to the park. "You can watch from here, Hastings."

"I won't be much help to Princess if that pit bull decides she's a plaything."

"Fine, just remember your job is the dog." Stu held the gate open for Jordan. Princess followed with Andrew still holding her leash. Andrew held open the second gate to the section of the park specified for small dogs, and Jordan released Princess to run around the empty park. On the side of the fence, the pit bull paced the area meant for larger dogs.

"I guess Princess doesn't need you to protect her." Stu sneered and walked to the tree where Andrew had hidden the bugs yesterday.

Andrew kept the bodyguard in his peripheral as he took Princess's ball out of his backpack.

Stu continued to circle the tree. He reached up and felt around a few times. He would need to jump to reach the listening devices. Andrew had a good four inches on the other bodyguard in height and more than that in reach. Stu lacked those extra few inches needed to find the bugs without having to climb the tree.

Jordan took the ball. "I hoped we could talk." She turned and tossed the ball.

Princess tired of fetching the ball after a few minutes and found a sunny spot to lie down. Jordan handed the ball back. "That must have been some jog you took her on this morning."

"Only 5k. I wasn't sure how much she could take."

Jordan laughed. "1k or less. Princess loves to walk, but running, not so much.

Stu joined them, his face grim. "Are you ready to go?"

Jordan checked her phone. "It's only been ten minutes."

"But your dog is just lying there."

"Princess is sunbathing. She needs the vitamin D to be healthy. Ten more minutes will not ruin anyone's schedule. The read-through isn't for another hour."

Stu stalked back to the tree he'd been examining.

Andrew stood behind the bench where Jordan sat. "Any chance Princess can be in the read-through with you for an hour? I'd like to take care of some things." It also gave him an excuse to stay near the hotel conference room where she should be.

"That could be a problem. I heard Storm is not a dog person. I found another bug."

It took a moment for Andrew to register what she added to the conversation. "Where?"

"Kitchen. If they aren't Stu's, I need to tell Paul. I need to practice my lines, and if it's an outsider recording me, it could be an issue."

Andrew assessed Stu's progress. "I think they are his. Either that or he saw me reach for something in the tree yesterday."

"If they can transmit that far, they'd be fairly boring to listen to. Birds, dogs, and squirrels." Jordan's contagious smile made it hard not to laugh.

Princess rolled over a few times, then came to sit by Jordan. She scratched the dog under the chin. "Too bad you're not a German Shepherd. We could pass notes in your little barrel."

"You mean Saint Bernard?" Andrew cleared his throat as Stu returned.

"Are you ready now?" snapped the bodyguard.

"I suppose so. Andrew, would you walk her around the trees before you come? I'd like to have her in with me today, and it won't work well if she's asking to go out all the time."

Stu folded his arms. "Paul won't like the dog being there."

Jordan didn't look up, instead rubbing the dog's belly and speaking in a singsong voice. "Princess is my emotional-support animal.

Last time I checked, I had a PTSD-worthy weekend. I'm sure he'll understand. Yes, he will, won't he Princess?" Jordan stood. "Andrew, will you bring her to my room at ten till?"

"Of course." Andrew leashed Princess to keep her from following Jordan out of the park, all the while reassessing Jordan's skills. She'd given him an excuse to stay in the park with all the other bodyguards gone and paved the way to have Princess in the read through. Perhaps he'd been too hasty last night and underestimated her.

She may be a woman of a dozen faces, but he was appreciating all of them. Andrew retrieved the bugs, planning on sending them to Alan for analysis.

Storm Tordon showed up forty-five minutes late to the reading, smelling of Thunder. Paul discreetly opened a window. Jordan hurried to bury her nose in Princess's fur. Thunder must have been engineered by a high school student trying to find a scent worse than old wet tennis shoes.

The reading progressed slowly. Storm demanded an explanation regarding everyone's motivation for almost every line. Jordan suppressed every natural emotion as Storm asked Suzi what the maid's motivation for straightening Princess Sam's closet was.

Behind a copy of her script, Reggie rolled her eyes and mouthed, "It was messy."

Paul grinned and nodded at Storm as if someone finally understood the director's point.

"I'm a maid. I clean things, and people pay me. And I report back to the King about what his daughter is really doing. My motivation is to listen in." The forty-something actress who played the maid and sometimes confidant didn't try to hide her annoyance.

Storm leaned forward, resting one arm on the table. "But is that enough?"

Princess growled.

Jordan interrupted. "Paul, I need to take Princess out. Can we take a fifteen-minute break?"

Storm pinned her with a glare. "We've only been working for an hour."

"Some of us have been here for nearly two." Jordan stood with Princess in her arms, wondering if she was a good enough actress to muster any on-stage chemistry with the narcissistic star. Of course, she could faint from the smell of Thunder and skip the kissing scenes. The thought of Storm attempting mouth-to-mouth was enough to convince Jordan to locate some smelling salts.

Paul checked his watch. "Hour break for everyone. Grab your lunches, people. And don't be late."

Stu and two other bodyguards waited outside the room. Andrew sat farther down at the end of the hall. Jordan made a beeline for him.

"Princess and I need some air." Jordan turned toward the door leading to the back parking lot and the small plot of grass marked for dog use.

Stu caught up with them. "Miss Lee, if you will please stay inside."

Jordan handed the leash to Andrew. "Please bring her up to my room when she's done?"

Andrew nodded. Jordan returned to her room and locked the bodyguards out after they checked it. She pulled a cereal box out of the cupboard, which was exactly how she'd left it, angled at forty-five degrees, and pulled her foil-wrapped phone out. It hadn't been until after Andrew dropped Princess off that she realized she'd normally left her phone with Blake. As the phone sprung to life, Jordan congratulated herself on finding a secure hiding place.

A text from her grandmother appeared. **Landed in London. Call me.**

There wasn't time to check for bugs, so Jordan opted for the balcony.

She opened the door and screamed.

"Aglet!"

THE ALERT FROM ANDREW'S PHONE came at the same time as the scream from the balcony above. He ran up the stairs to Jordan's room, Princess tucked under an arm like a football.

A bodyguard came out of the room across the hall. "What was that?"

Andrew tapped his phone on the lock, hoping Blake's app could unlock the door. The light turned green, and he pushed the door open. Jordan stood next to the balcony door, hand to her throat. Princess barked. He set the dog down, her leash still tethered to his carabiner.

"Don't let her out there." Jordan got the last word out as Andrew wrapped an arm around her waist and pulled her deeper into the room.

"Get your hands off her!" The bodyguard he'd passed in the hall held out a taser.

Would the guy be dumb enough to use it while Andrew was holding Jordan?

Jordan pointed to the balcony. "Out there." The guard moved his focus.

Andrew walked Jordan to the hallway, Princess following. Another bodyguard came out of the room where the first had been. The first shouted from the balcony, and the second ran toward the noise. Andrew pulled Jordan into the safest place he could think of—the guards' room—and closed the door. He spun Jordan to face him. "What happened?"

Jordan closed her eyes and took a deep breath. "An old photo—with a knife through it." She stepped closer and leaned her head against his chest. Her entire body was shaking as if she'd just done a polar-bear plunge. "A-a photo...of my...my mom."

Andrew pulled her closer. Princess barked as the door burst open, and Andrew pushed Jordan behind him.

The incompetent guard held up an 8 x 10 glossy smeared with what looked like ketchup. "It's just some prank."

Jordan buried her head in Andrew's back. Princess jumped up on his legs.

"Put that photo away. You shouldn't have moved it. It is evidence."

Stu entered the room. "What's evidence?"

"Just a prank, boss." The guard held out the photo.

Stu's jaw formed a hard line. He turned to someone behind him. "Find us a secure room. And lock down Jordan's." He pointed to the incompetent guard. "You, in the hall now, and you too," Stu directed the guard who'd been standing in the center of the room when Andrew entered.

Stu slammed the door behind them. "What happened?"

Jordan lifted her head from Andrew's back and stepped out far enough to scoop up her dog. "I went to make a private call. Since I keep finding bugs in the room, I decided to call from the balcony. I opened the door and saw the photo, then screamed. Andrew got there first. That guy"—Jordan pointed to the empty spot where the guard who'd held the photo had stood—"pulled a taser on us. Andrew got me in here. Your bodyguard with the photo came in."

Stu looked to Andrew for confirmation.

Andrew stayed between Stu and Jordan. "I assumed since the

guards were in here, this was the safest room. Why didn't you have someone escort Miss Lee to her room?"

"We did. Rod checked the room. He must have missed the balcony."

Andrew hoped his impassive guard face was firmly in place. He refrained from asking stupid questions like why Stu hadn't done the job himself. "Your crime scene has been compromised by your own men. This is the second time in thirty-six hours Miss Lee has received a threat in an area that should have been secured. You call the police now, or I will."

Stu pulled out his phone. The call to a detective was brief. "They're sending someone over."

Andrew steered Jordan to the cleanest of the empty chairs around a table littered with the remains of an interrupted card game. No one spoke. Andrew didn't because he didn't want to ask his questions in front of Stu. Jordan kept her gaze down as she played with Princess, who sat in her lap.

Mr. Blake had alluded to people bringing up her parents' disappearance from time to time. Every once in a while, a real-life-mystery television show would revisit how the plane carrying Hirst and Ellen Lee had disappeared and how their daughter had been left behind.

A couple of minutes later, Paul entered the room. Jordan tightened her grip on Andrew's arm.

"Jordan, I need you downstairs now. You are already five minutes late. We can't wait all day. Storm is getting impatient."

Sirens wailed outside the window now. Stu cleared his throat. "That's the police. Jordan will be a few minutes longer."

"Why?" Paul glared at Jordan.

She leaned back in her chair and scratched the dog's ears. "Someone left me a rather unpleasant surprise. I think I should talk to the police since we've called them, don't you?" Her voice was calm to the point of boredom. Andrew wondered what character Jordan was channeling for this scene. What an interesting coping mechanism. When the going got tough, Jordan got acting.

Paul's face reddened. "Fine, just get down there as soon as you can. We are behind schedule," he said, narrowly avoiding a collision with the police officer in the doorway as he stormed out.

Jordan stood and handed Princess to Andrew before shaking the officer's hand. The calm, factual Jordan from the hospital room was back. Since no one asked him to leave, Andrew stayed to listen in as she explained she hadn't seen anyone. As soon as she'd realized what she was seeing, she'd screamed, and the bodyguards had come running. She didn't mention that she'd specifically contacted Andrew. It could have been an automatic response if she'd used her panic word for years.

"Who was the first to arrive?" asked the officer.

Jordan looked at Andrew.

"And what did you see?"

"Miss Lee was standing two feet back from the sliding glass door. I pulled her farther into the room. She indicated there was something on the balcony, so I removed her from the area as quickly as possible. Two of the Hearthfire bodyguards came into the suite as we were leaving. A minute or two later, one of them returned with a photo."

The officer looked at Andrew's gray button-down shirt, then at Stu's Hearthfire shirt. "Are you a bodyguard too?"

Stu stepped forward. "Mr. Hastings's job is to protect Princess, the dog."

"Like the man who saved Miss Lee at the airport. Interesting. So who's supposed to protect Miss Lee?"

THE SIX-HOUR CHICAGO-TO-LONDON TIME DIFFERENCE was easy enough to compute on the slow-moving wall clock. Jordan wondered how early she could ask for the session to end. Storm had moved away from the motivation questions when the actor playing her bodyguard said something about punching someone and glared. Paul had to call a ten-minute break, and soon. So far, the only person other than Paul who could tolerate Storm was Kittie. The stand-in read September's parts as well as other minor females'. Kittie Morse answered each question more creatively and gave Storm a veneered smile that must have cost her parents a pretty penny.

It was now 10:00 p.m. in London. Could they quit already? She needed to tell Grandma about the incident on the patio before Andrew turned in his report and Blake relayed it to London.

Halfway through the next page, Storm stood. "I have dinner reservations. Jordan, will you join me?"

"No, I have an appointment of my own."

Paul shot Jordan a look. "Can't you rearrange?"

Jordan used her best Claire Lee impression. "I'm afraid not. They have discharged Blake from the hospital, and he's leaving in the morning. I promised I would say goodbye. He saved my life."

Storm appraised the rest of the women in the room. When his gaze landed on Reggie, she shook her head. "Um, uh, my boyfriend told me to stay far away from you."

Kittie practically jumped up and down trying to get his attention, but Storm shrugged and left the room. Jordan felt for the girl, but right now she needed to get to her phone. She waved and hurried to the door, where she was met by Stu and Rod. Andrew stood at the end of the hall with Princess. Jordan headed for the dog. Her phone was in Princess's vest, right where she'd left it. Andrew raised an eyebrow as she slipped it out of the vest and into her pocket. "Have you been a good girl?" Jordan scratched the dog's ears.

"She mostly slept."

"I assume she needs a walk." Jordan turned to Stu. "Blake and I used to go to random neighborhoods. He said it was safest as no one could plan ahead. He would walk with me and have someone shadow us in a car. Would that work?"

"How did he choose the neighborhood?"

"Off a real-estate map. Blake chose middle-class neighborhoods. If the neighborhood is too wealthy, they get suspicious of strangers. No one in a middle-class neighborhood has a clue who their neighbors are because they're always at work or soccer."

Stu nodded. "That sounds reasonable."

"I need to change my shoes." Jordan searched Stu's face. After the police left, he'd promised to keep an eye on her room. Paul still refused to have her move to a different hotel or a rental. And other than changing rooms with someone else, there weren't many options. "Come on, Princess, help me choose my walking shoes."

As she hoped, Andrew followed her. Stu didn't stop him. At the room, she let Princess and Andrew in first. She hoped it wasn't obvious that she trusted his skills more than the guards hired to keep her safe.

The neighborhood Stu found was perfectly suited to walking

a dog. Andrew walked on the outside of the sidewalk, alert to everything. Jordan slipped her earbuds in.

"I need to call my grandmother. Can you do me a favor and make it look like we are talking and not really listen in?"

"I'll do my best."

"Thanks." Jordan dialed. "Hi, Grandma, sorry it's so late. We were running a read-through that went forever. How was your flight?"

"You know how it is. I'm just glad to land someplace I can call home." Of the three European properties Grandma owned, the London apartment was Jordan's favorite.

"I need to tell you I've had a bit more excitement here."

"Other than the shooting?"

"A black rose in a box by my hotel room door, and someone left a photo of Mom with ketchup on it and a steak knife through it on my balcony."

Claire Lee swore in French, Swedish, and German. "Pardon my language, dear. Isn't that new bodyguard of yours any good?"

Jordan snuck a side glance at Andrew, who whispered the words to *Mary Had a Little Lamb* keeping up the pretense that she was talking to him. "He is the one who got me out of danger both times. He has a plan for getting a second person on to his team."

"How's Blake?"

"They released him today. His wife is here to take him back to LA. I will go visit them tonight."

"So you think you are safe with Andrew?"

"Yes, I do."

A yawn came from the London end of the line. "I wish I could talk longer, but my body has no idea what time it is, and my clock says I have call time in eight hours. Love you, bunny."

"I love you too."

"Tell that young man to take good care of you." Claire's voice faded.

"Don't worry. He does. Bye."

Andrew's eyebrows raised during the last part of the conversation, but he didn't ask any questions when she hung up. "Can we have a real conversation for a second?"

"Sure."

"September is going to bring the best dog whisperer in Chicago with her when she comes up Thursday afternoon."

"That long?" Forty-some odd hours was a very long time.

"Sorry. It couldn't be faster."

"I was hoping to get some sleep. I'm a little nervous since this afternoon. I did get my pass key card changed."

"Can I copy it to my phone?" Andrew pulled his phone out of his pocket and brought up Blake's app. Jordan pressed her keycard to the phone. Stu's car inched closer.

"I wish I could keep Princess in my room, but if she needs to go out in the night, I have to wake up half the hotel."

"If you can't sleep tonight, you can call me and pretend I'm some friend from home. I promise you a conversation so boring that whoever is listening through the bugs will ignore it."

"You would do that for me?"

"My job is your safety. If you aren't sleeping, you aren't safe. If I can bore you into slumber, I will." Andrew smiled as he made the offer. As if talking to him could be boring.

"What if our conversation keeps me up?" Jordan couldn't resist teasing Andrew, hoping for another smile.

"I will read the dictionary to you."

Stu drove up next to them. "Walk is over now."

Jordan bent down to scratch Princess behind the ears before handing her leash to Andrew. "See you soon." She hoped he realized she meant him too.

Stu said Princess can stay up here tonight as long as I text him if she needs to go outside.

Jordan's text had been a surprise. Andrew took the dog outside before heading to the elevator. When the elevator opened, Andrew found Stu waiting inside. He joined the bodyguard and pushed the button for the third floor.

Stu inserted a key that kept the elevator from opening on other floors. "How many bugs did you find?"

"I believe the total is six now. Are all of them yours?"

"Only four, including the two still in the room. I didn't break her contract. As long as they aren't in her private areas, we can use any means necessary to protect her."

Andrew didn't respond. "Where did the other two come from?"

"I don't know. I checked her room when she went to dinner and only found ours."

"Would you like me to do a sweep?"

"Yes, we have one on the back of the lamp next to the couch and one in the kitchen behind the coffee maker." Stu pressed the elevator's stop button. "I don't like what's going on any more than you do. I didn't get to hire my own team, and I have some of the biggest nitwits in the industry working for me."

Andrew didn't hide his momentary smile. "How come she can't have her own security team and a nice little rental that's easier to guard?"

"I don't know. This whole mess is new to me. Managing the lot is much easier given access points, employee IDs, and full background checks. Shooting at the mansion they chose will be a nightmare. The grounds are huge, there's even a garden maze, and supposedly the house was built in 1870, complete with hidden passages because the owner was paranoid. And the current owner won't give us a blueprint to anyplace other than the rooms we're shooting in."

"I heard Mr. Tordon is staying there."

"Only in the guesthouse. We're not filming there. I need you on-site as much as possible. I don't like that this is happening on my watch."

In other words, Stu wasn't going to take the blame. Andrew nodded. "I'll do my best, but try to give me as much access as possible. Do you want your bugs back?"

"The ones you removed from the room or the ones in there?"

"Either?"

"I'm assuming you destroyed the first two. Don't bother. But leave the two in there and let me know if you find any others." Stu restarted the elevator.

"Spying on her isn't the same as protecting her. You should remove your other ones too." Jordan couldn't relax if she knew someone listened to everything she did.

Andrew made a quick check of the room with Jordan trailing behind. He didn't find any bugs not belonging to Hearthfire. He signed to Jordan the relevant parts of his conversation with Stu.

"My contract?" Jordan's signing reflected her anger. "I'll have my a-g-e-n-t check." She finger-spelled *agent*, which was a good thing since Andrew wasn't sure of the sign for it either.

"Remember, call me if you need to."

"I will."

The first call came an hour later.

"Did you know they have a channel for dogs to watch?"

Andrew didn't.

It turned out the humans found the show more entertaining than Princess did.

They watched an old eighties sitcom for a half hour before Jordan said she was tired enough to fall asleep.

The second call came at 2:00 a.m.

Jordan cried and hiccupped between each syllable. If it hadn't been for caller ID, Andrew would have hung up on the incoherent babel.

Andrew wished he could climb the stairs to her room. "Bad dream?"

"Y-y-es. I dream-med I was on-n the plane with them. It's always the same."

Them not him. Her parents and not the shooting with Blake. "What do you do to get back to sleep?"

"Hold Princess, drink hot chocolate."

Andrew turned on the lights. "Do you have any hot chocolate?"

"No."

From the depths of his go-bag, Andrew pulled two packets of instant cocoa. "I have two packages. It isn't the good stuff, but you can use the coffee maker in your room to make some."

"How can I get it?"

"Ring Stu. I'll be up to get Princess in a minute."

"I need her back."

Andrew closed the door to his apartment. "I know."

Jordan pulled a sweatshirt over her cami top and called Stu. He answered on the fourth ring.

"What?"

"Mr. Andrew is coming to take Princess out, and I need her back."

"I'll tell the guard."

The line went dead.

Princess remained curled up on the bed. Jordan waited by the door for Andrew. She opened the door on the first knock, letting Andrew in but keeping Rod out. A shiver ran up her spine.

Andrew pulled two crumpled packets of hot cocoa from his back pocket. "Sorry it isn't a better brand."

She took them without touching him. "For the middle of the night, these are perfect." Jordan avoided looking Andrew in the eyes, knowing that if she did, the tears would start again. A light touch on her shoulder broke her resolve, his face becoming blurry through her tears.

He opened his arms, and she fell into them, wrapping her arms around his chest. No words passed as they stood there. Someone tapped at the door, and Jordan pulled back. "Coming."

"Are you going to be okay?"

Jordan shrugged. It was the most honest answer she could give. "This will help."

"Where is Princess?"

Another knock.

"On my bed," signed Jordan.

Andrew signed back. "Do you want me to take her out or tell Rod it was a false alarm?"

I want you to stay here. Not going to happen for so many reasons. "Take her out. A false alarm will only make them suspicious."

Andrew shifted his weight. "Will you go get her?"

More knocking.

Jordan hurried to her room and scooped up Princess. Andrew waited near the coffee table with the leash. Princess's ears perked up.

"Come on, girl. Let's see if you're as good an actress as your owner."

Jordan shut the door behind them, walked into the kitchen, and pulled down two mugs. Reluctantly, she put one back. As much as she wanted company, she knew Andrew wouldn't stay when he brought Princess back, even if Rod wasn't knocking on the door every ten seconds.

Andrew carried Princess back up in the elevator and found Rod and Stu waiting outside Jordan's room.

"No need to go in this time," said Stu as he knocked on Jordan's door.

Andrew set the dog down and handed Jordan the leash.

"Thanks."

"Anytime."

Stu put his foot inside Jordan's door. "Next time, make the handoff quicker. Paul asked me to remind you that your contract forbids males in your room late at night."

"Tell Paul I'm aware of my contract." Jordan nodded and glared at Stu's shoe.

Andrew heard the dead bolt slide into place and turned to leave.

"Not so fast, Hastings. Rod said you were in the room for over ten minutes and we didn't pick up anything on our sound." The folded arms and wide stance Stu meant to intimidate Andrew with fell short of its desired goal.

"It takes a while to communicate when one doesn't want to be overheard. Remove the bugs, Stu. Miss Lee has a right to privacy in the entire suite." Not waiting for a response, Andrew headed for the stairwell.

Once he was in his room, he texted Jordan.

Have a good night.

—Thanks for the hot chocolate.

Anytime.

He meant it more than he should.

For the second night in a row, Jordan dialed Andrew's number. She'd anticipated calling him all day. Last night's first conversation was unlike any experience she'd ever had. For two hours she hadn't worried about how she looked in her pajama pants, T-shirt, and messy bun or how she sounded, even to whoever was listening in. His response to her second call was everything a knight-in-shining-armor response should have been.

At lunch today, he'd handed her a grocery bag filled with three different varieties of hot-cocoa mix. Jordan hit the button to call Andrew.

"Hello, Princess." Andrew's deep voice sent shivers down her spine.

"She can't come to the phone right now."

"Sorry. I binge-watched the rest of season one of *The Adventures of Princess Sam* while you were in your read-through today."

"No, you didn't!" Jordan hugged her pillow to her chest.

"Not much else to do other than watch your dog sleep. We established that the doggy channel was not entertaining."

"It could be argued season one isn't entertaining either."

"Au contraire. Princess Sam and the rainforest was very entertaining."

Jordan caught her reflection in the mirror. Thank goodness Andrew couldn't see her blushing. On film, that shade of red needed makeup enhancement. "New topic, please?"

They'd talked for the next two hours and watched one of her grandma's most famous movies on the oldies cable channel together from their own rooms. Princess whined at the door. "I think Princess needs you."

"I'll be right up. Let Stu know."

Jordan dashed into the bathroom and redid her bun and checked to make sure her T-shirt didn't have chocolate dribbled down the front. "Where's your leash?"

Her heart jumped at the knock on the door. She checked through the peephole before opening it for Andrew. Princess danced around his feet. "Someone is excited to see me."

Their fingers brushed as Jordan handed him the leash. Two someones were excited to see him.

Princess raced Andrew down the stairs and to the area of grass specified for dog use. When she finished, she nudged Andrew's leg to propel him back into the building. He understood the dog's excitement. After two hours on the phone, he wanted to get back to talking to Jordan too.

Stu stood guard in the hallway outside Jordan's door. "Ten minutes." He spoke so low Andrew almost missed it.

He knocked on the door, and Jordan opened it immediately. Princess bounded in, Andrew close behind. As soon as Jordan shut the door, Andrew signed, "Stu said ten minutes. Do you want me to search for new bugs?"

"I don't care. But will you make sure the balcony is secure?" she signed back.

Andrew nodded and checked all the rooms and windows. Stu's bugs were no longer on the lamp or in the kitchen. Jordan curled up in one of the big chairs with her feet under her and Princess in her lap.

"All clear," he signed.

Jordan spoke. "Thanks. You have six minutes left. Will you sit down for a minute?"

Andrew sat in the chair opposite her.

"How do you think he got in to leave the photo on the balcony?"

He frowned before answering. "You shouldn't think about this right before bed."

"I know. But no one is telling me anything."

"My guess is the front door." Andrew had checked the roof. There was no evidence of anyone having rappelled down. "I'm glad you're keeping Princess up here tonight. She'll growl if anyone tries to get in."

"I know. I think she is an actress. Her bark belongs to a Doberman. You're sure she won't need to go out?" His raised brows, indicated the question was about more than just the dog.

Jordan pointed to herself. "I'm sure Princess will be fine tonight."

Andrew laughed and stood. "I'd better go."

Jordan pushed Princess off her lap and stood to see him to the door.

"You'll lock up behind me?"

"Of course." She touched his arm.

His feet stopped, but his heart sped up.

Jordan stepped closer, her whispered breath brushing his cheek. "Can I call you if I can't sleep?"

"Anytime."

"Thanks." Jordan stepped back, leaving a void.

Andrew listened for the dead bolt to set before walking down the stairs and waiting for a phone call he knew he should not be anticipating.

BUILT IN THE MID-EIGHTIES, THE movie studio wasn't as big as the one they used in LA, but it was better equipped than what Jordan expected for Green Bay. Set designers unloaded pieces as familiar as her own home from several semitrucks.

Paul yelled at everyone about losing a day of shooting. "The sets should have been put up yesterday. Move it, move it!" The crew muttered. They couldn't help it if the trucks were late.

Jordan escaped to her trailer to wait for the new call time. Andrew and Princess joined her.

"Do you always get trailers on set?" Andrew let Princess do some exploring.

"Not all the time, but with a lack of dressing rooms and the fact that they can move this to the mansion for those shots, it makes it so I don't have to move all my stuff."

"Stuff?"

"Look in the bedroom. I think a third of my wardrobe is in there."

Andrew stuck his head into the back room. "I didn't realize being a princess required so many clothes."

"Wait until you see my wedding dress. They designed a twelve-foot train. Kate Middleton's only had a nine-foot train, and she is really a royal. Needless to say, it won't fit in the trailer. My ball gowns aren't in there either." Jordan frowned.

"You don't like ball gowns? Even my sister Abbie likes to play dress up."

"Not so much the gowns as the scenes I have to do in them. One gown is strapless, daring by Hearthfire standards, and I have to dance with Storm. I don't know how I can pretend to have chemistry with him when he is touching my bare back. And if he wears Thunder, I might ruin the front of his tux. Wardrobe won't be happy about that."

Andrew sat on the arm of the couch. "You don't like him much, do you?"

"No, and it will cause problems. We have three kissing scenes. First kiss, engagement, and wedding. Paul is filming the first next week. He was going to do them all the last week of filming, but I think he hopes Storm will wow me and we will get some better on-screen chemistry." Jordan made a gagging noise and a barfing sign. Andrew laughed.

Someone knocked on the door. Andrew opened it to find Storm.

"Scram, bodyguard. Princess Sam and I need to have a talk."

Princess growled and advanced on Storm, her tail stiff. Jordan gagged as the scent of Thunder filled the room.

"And take her mutt with you."

Princess barked.

Jordan made the sign for shoes, and Andrew gave the slightest of nods. Jordan stood and scooped up Princess, who continued to growl, and sat at the far end of the couch. "Storm, come in and have a seat." She pointed to the chair farthest from her.

"Have him take the dog out of here."

Jordan stroked Princess's head. "If they leave, she will bark so loud that everyone on the lot will come running. Princess has been very jumpy since the shooting, so if you want to speak to me, you'll have to do it with both her and Andrew here."

Storm scowled and plopped down on the couch. "We need to work on our chemistry. Everyone noticed in the reading."

Jordan scooted as far as she could away from Storm as he laid his arm across the cushion backs. "If we start the film off with too much chemistry, we'll ruin the meet cute."

"We don't film our first meeting until day ten. What about the first kiss? We film that on day six. The audience won't buy it if you aren't into me."

"Princess Sam has not been kissed since her coming-out ball when she kissed her first love, whom she's pining for. An awkward kiss will be perfect for the scene." If only the actor who played her first love wasn't involved in a mega-blockbuster series and could get away to film the finale.

"I've studied your screen kisses. They lack passion."

"All my kisses are exactly what the director and ratings call for. Remember, these kisses are for a Hearthfire audience. Sweet, wholesome, and heartwarming. Not all hot and bothered, like in the movies you do."

Storm scoffed. "They're probably the only kisses you know how to do. It's true, isn't it? Not one picture anywhere of you in an off-screen smooch."

Jordan petted Princess, wishing the dog would do more than growl. "And this has what to do with our show?"

"I'm not convinced you can make it work. If this flops and I lose credibility because my female audience thinks I'm not a good kisser because of your poor acting, I'll ruin you." Storm leaned in, and Princess lunged between them and growled.

"Any woman who has smelled Thunder will know our less-than-passionate kisses are because I'm holding my breath."

"How fast do you want your career to tank?"

Andrew stood near Storm's end of the couch. If Jordan said the word, Storm would be out of the trailer as fast as her career if she kicked the star out. Storm had the connections to make good on his threat. But then, Jordan had decent connections of her own, not to mention Grandma's.

"I'm an actress. Don't worry. No one will know that I can't stand the sight or smell of you." Taking him on wasn't her usual style. This week was already on record as one of the worst of her life. Storm would have to have all of Hollywood wired to make good on his threat, and being this year's most eligible actor wasn't enough to do that.

Storm lifted his arm from the back of the couch and pointed at her nose. "Prove it."

Jordan scratched Princess's ears, trying to calm the growling dog. "I will next week on set."

"Not good enough. Prove it now, or I'll walk. Or fly right back to LA."

"I want our first kiss to be authentic. If I kiss you now, I could ruin it and end up laughing during the take or something."

"You say you can do what the director tells you?"

"Of course."

"Fine." Storm's smile took on a wicked twist as he stood and moved to sit down in the chair across from the couch. He inclined his head toward Andrew. "Then kiss him as I direct."

"That is not appropriate. Mr. Hastings and I have a professional relationship, and he isn't an actor." Jordan signed a quick "sorry."

"He's a red-blooded man, isn't he? Believe me. He won't mind."

"This is way outside of his contract."

"Kiss him or I walk." Storm stood, emphasizing his threat.

Jordan signed "help" and hoped it looked like she was petting Princess. Andrew signed back, "O-k" and tapped his closed fingers against his cheek to sign "kiss."

"So, Princess, are you going to kiss him, or do I walk?" sneered Storm.

Jordan put out her hand. "I'll do it. But if I do, you will not wear Thunder on any day we are scheduled to have a scene together."

"You hate it that much?" The surprised look on Storm's face tempted Jordan to giggle. "Fine. I won't wear it on the set when we're supposed to be together." Storm clapped his hands. "Let's get started."

"Hand over your cell phone. This is a closed set."

Storm smirked and pulled the latest-model phone from his pocket. "I wouldn't film it anyway. I don't need lessons."

Jordan pocketed his phone. "Fine. Get directing."

"Princess Sam, you stay there. Big guy, sit on this end of the couch. I know you aren't an actor, so Princess Sam will do all the work."

Jordan set her dog on the floor and signaled for her to go lie down on her pillow under the table.

Storm sat in one of the chairs and leaned forward. "Now, Princess Sam, this is how this kiss is going to go. You will crawl along the couch to the big man here. Keep your eyes on his. He needs to know what's coming. The kiss of a lifetime. You are sexy, like a sleek cat. When you reach him, you will straddle his lap, frame his face with your hands, then kiss him long and sensual. I want to feel you wanting him."

"But this is a first kiss!" She had zero experience with the type of kiss Storm demanded.

"No, Princess, this is acting. Prove to me you can act, or I tell Paul I'm done."

Jordan closed her eyes and took a breath. She didn't want to kiss Andrew like this. If she ever kissed him, she wanted it to be real.

Storm cleared his throat. Jordan opened her eyes and sought Andrew's. *I'm sorry, I'm sorry.* She leaned forward and crawled toward Andrew as directed. Climbing onto his lap wasn't as easily accomplished, but she did it. Slipping one hand behind his head. Her lips met his. He didn't move. Jordan pressed her lips to his and slowly mouthed "I'm sorry" against his lips before pulling back.

"Adequate. I'll stay—and look forward to our first kiss." Storm patted her behind, removing his phone from her back pocket, and left the trailer to Princess's growling.

Jordan slid off Andrew's lap and blinked back tears. "I'm so sorry." Then she escaped into the bedroom, closed the thin door between them, slid to the floor, and let the tears flow.

Andrew wiped the kiss from his mouth. So that was acting? It was the least enjoyable kiss of his life.

He should have done something other than give Jordan the go-ahead. Forcing her to kiss him was wrong. Even if he wasn't the one doing the forcing. He moved to the bedroom door and tapped.

"Jordan? I'm sure you can hear me. I'm sorry. I shouldn't have let you go through with it. I let him bully you. I'm sorry. I really am." Andrew leaned his head against the door. There was no way to fix this. He couldn't erase the last ten minutes.

The door vibrated against his forehead and opened an inch. Jordan wrapped her fingers around it, holding it mostly closed. "I should have let him walk. If I told HR what he threatened me with, they would have sided with me."

Andrew covered her hand with his. "I'm sorry. I should have told him to take a hike."

One watery amber eye met his for a second before her eyelid shuttered it. "It's not your fault. I feel like I betrayed our friendship. I don't have many friends. It is hard to have friends when they're in the same cutthroat business." Jordan lowered her voice to a whisper. "I thought last night, if I ever kissed you it would be my first kiss with a real person. I mean not an actor, and I ruined that. You can never get a second first kiss."

"You've never kissed for real?"

"I don't know. They've all been actors." The thin door shook as Jordan gave a strangled laugh. "Every kiss has been for the camera or director. Even my first boyfriend only kissed me when the paparazzi snapped photos. I don't know why Storm didn't find those. Anyway, kissing for the camera made me question what was real. Since then, I've limited public kissing to the cheek. And private to when I'm fairly sure he isn't using me as a wrung on his ladder to stardom. And that never happens. I won't date a leading man until three months after shooting is complete. They all move on by then, so I don't kiss much. I've hoped that someday I will find someone I can be real with. Last night when we were laughing over that cat video, I thought—" Her voice dissolved in tears.

Andrew wished the door away so he could comfort her. It wouldn't help for him to point out how he'd wondered what it would be like to hold her hand during the movie they'd watched together from their respective rooms. Andrew waited for the sobs to quiet. "It may not matter, but I didn't kiss you. I'm fairly sure a good kiss takes two. If we were to kiss, it would be my first time kissing you, and that would be real."

Jordan pulled the door open enough that half of her face appeared. The tears had smeared her eye makeup. "You're sure? Don't answer that. I don't want to ruin our friendship." She closed her eyes. "Pretend I didn't ask."

"Ask what?"

Her eyes opened, the tears receding. "I understand if you need to quit. After what you explained about Adam and September."

"I'm not quitting over a directed kiss. Although, I can see how you might want to fire me. I didn't do a very good job of protecting you."

"You did. You didn't leave me, and as difficult as it was to act with you, it would have been worse if he had forced me to kiss him. He would have taken advantage and made it—"

Someone pounded on the trailer door. "Ten minutes to call, Miss Lee!"

"Thank you!" shouted Jordan.

"You should probably fix your makeup."

Jordan's hands flew to her face. "Oh!" She turned from the door and stopped. "Will you stay and walk me to the set? I need Storm to see we are normal. He can never know that I—that I lost it."

"I'll wait."

Andrew checked the mirror next to the door and cleaned the smeared red lip-gloss from around his mouth. Jordan emerged from the bedroom with only the faintest pink around her eyes.

"Do I look okay?"

"Always."

Jordan laughed. "I know it's one of those trick questions. Right up there with 'Does this dress make me look fat?'"

Her jeans did not make her look the least bit fat. Andrew swallowed and looked away. "My brother-in-law told me to never, ever answer that question."

"Good thing I'm not wearing a dress."

"Do you need a hug? I mean, friends hug …" Andrew shoved his hands in his pockets as he felt the heat in his face rise.

"Really? I could use a hug."

Andrew pulled his hands out and opened his arms. Jordan walked into the hug and wrapped her arms around his waist. Andrew closed his arms and breathed in her peachy fragrance. Princess yipped and jumped on their legs, her tail wagging. After a few counts, he dropped his arms.

Jordan stepped back. "We're good?"

"Better than good. We are friends."

SEPTEMBER AND ADAM STOOD NEAR the entrance of the studio, looking like they should be the lead characters in a Hearthfire movie. He even wore a plaid shirt. Two Hastings security guards in navy blue polos stood a discreet distance away with a woman in jeans and an I heart dogs t-shirt. As Jordan approached, the couple broke apart, and September engulfed Jordan in a hug.

"I brought that magical dog person I told you about. She'll get Princess back to her old self in no time." The medium-sized brunette stepped forward and stood next to September, who made the introductions. "This is Tonie. She's a wiz with dogs."

A polite shaking of hands followed.

Acting. This Jordan could do. "Thank you. I've been so worried. Princess won't touch her kibble at all." Not a lie. Princess didn't like dry dog food.

The door of the studio opened, and Kittie, in her stocking cap, whistled one shrill note. "Hey, in here for the meeting."

"I'll wait out here. Mr. Andrew can introduce me to your dog," said Tonie.

Andrew leaned in close to Jordan's ear. "You got this. Adam will keep an eye on you."

September caught Jordan's arm. "Let's go hear what's going on."

The cast and crew gathered around the grand-stairway set. Paul stood three steps up. "No show is without its problems, but it seems this one is starting out full of them. They rerouted a truck carrying the rest of the sets to Kalamazoo, and they won't be here until this afternoon or evening. I've had the set designers go through the ones we have here, and apparently we are missing something from every set other than the dining room. Since the main scene for that room requires Claire Lee's cameo, we won't be able to shoot today. September, my apologies, but we can't shoot the Christmas Tree song today. We should be able to do it tomorrow. I'll email out the rest of the changes. We'll film on Saturday to make up for the lost day. Questions?"

No one spoke.

"Cast, please practice your lines. Crew, let's finish getting things unloaded."

September linked her arm through Jordan's. "Come with us. Adam's promised me the best cheese curd in the state."

Jordan found Stu among the milling crowd. "I'm going with September. She has a full entourage of Hastings Security guards with her."

"Is Andrew going with you too?"

"I assume so. I'll be taking Princess." *Please don't send Hearth-fire guards.*

"Check in when you get back." Stu dismissed them with a wave.

September gave Adam a thumbs-up. "Ride with me. Adam and Andrew can meet us there."

"What about Princess?"

"Look, Tonie has her." September slid into the back seat of an SUV, Jordan following her. A driver and another guard got in the front. September leaned forward. "Can we have the privacy window up? I'm going to talk about your boss, and I know you don't want to hear how good of a kisser he is."

Both guards laughed, and the automatic privacy window rolled up between the front and back seats.

"Do you embarrass your bodyguards often?"

"More often than I should. When Adam is with me, he isn't on duty, so sometimes I slip and there's some PDA. Not much, but they still have to work with each other, and no one wants to witness his boss kissing in the back seat. We are going to go to the house I rented. After Saturday, I wasn't going to bring Harmony up here to the hotel. Adam pointed out it gives you a backup safe house. We haven't told Hearthfire where we are. They don't need to know either. Now spill. I want to know what brought you to tears this morning. Your eyes don't lie. I know you were crying."

Jordan studied the dividing window. "Storm put me in an awkward position with Andrew..."

"What exactly did Storm do?"

"It was so stupid. I should have seen it coming. I was trying to avoid kissing Storm off set, and I got forced into letting him direct me in a kiss with Andrew. Storm said if I didn't, he'd walk. Of course, he directed a predatory kiss on my part, and—" Jordan swiped at the new tears forming.

"Is Andrew a bad kisser?"

"I don't... know. He didn't move. Didn't participate. Just sat there. I'm not sure if that makes it worse or not. But I'm glad he didn't take advantage of the situation. He could have pushed it further. I feel like I violated something precious. And he's the one trying to tell me it's okay."

"Could he be right?" prodded September.

"I think he thinks he is. But I don't know. And how stupid is this? I'm crying over a guy I've known for five days. Mostly because when we talk, he talks to me as a person, not someone he needs something from. And Andrew is super hot, which makes things confusing because for once I'm not faking the chemistry. I feel like we were starting to be friends, even with the bodyguard distancing thing. And there were a couple moments when I thought there could be something more. The first time, I couldn't believe those kinds of things happened in real life. I waited for the director to yell 'Cut!' but then realized it was real. I'm sure the kiss ruined any could-have-beens."

"Andrew is a Hastings. He doesn't have a choice but to be hot. I blame the parents." September smiled a gushy smile, meaning she wasn't thinking about Andrew.

"Not helping."

"Sorry. Amazingly for Hollywood, you have avoided toxic relationships—especially with your costars—other than the one you made me promise never to talk about. Why now?"

"Grandma says it's the knight-in-shining armor thing. I've met nice guys before, including actors. Did you know when I worked with Kirk, he got the director to change our kissing scene so I wouldn't be as embarrassed? Not once have I even had an inkling of a crush on any of them. Andrew and I connect. Seriously, I have talked with him more this week than any other guy, excluding Blake, in the past three years."

September produced a box of tissues from the side of her seat. "That's how those Hastings boys got me. For about a week when I was sixteen, I had a crush on Andrew, then one on Alex. I guess that's how I knew when Adam came along that it wasn't just a crush. He's ten years older than I am, and he tried to treat me like a kid sister. There were a couple times I thought I would strangle him. Then, one day, he saw me. The real me. Not the singer, not the kid sister, not the principal he guarded. Me. We never talked about it and never acknowledged what was happening. We just kept skirting around the subject. That's why our first kiss sent us both running. I know my fans try to blame him for everything that happened, but it took two. I didn't take responsibility for my part until after things spun out of control, but if I had been honest then, maybe Adam would have been my husband last year and Harmony would have his eyes."

"What are you trying to tell me?"

"I don't know. Trust Andrew. I can vouch that he's one of the good guys. And trust your heart and be true to it. Keep letting the friendship grow. If this kiss of sorts makes things awkward, tell him. And remember, he wouldn't have participated in Storm's scene if he didn't think it was something you needed."

They pulled up to a modern box-style house.

"So how do I face him again?" asked Jordan.

"The way you always do. Smiling."

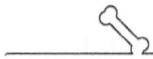

"Mom's here?" Andrew blanched. He could hide his emotions from Adam, but Mom was a different story. She should have worked for the CIA with her knack for ferreting out secrets.

Adam shrugged. "Harmony's nanny called in sick this morning, and Harmony is cutting teeth. Mom's the only person qualified to love Harmony in the middle of the grouchiest day ever and protect her if needed."

"Doesn't that violate the whole don't-protect-someone-you-love thing?" Not a rule Andrew felt qualified to define.

"Mom claims the rule doesn't apply to grandmas."

"Can you imagine the person who tries to touch or harm Harmony?"

"The entire comic-book universe wouldn't have a character who could stand up to Mom in that case."

Andrew laughed. "Remember when you asked me to sneak into Mom and Dad's room to find her magic bracelets? I was so convinced Mom was a superhero, I didn't dare lie for weeks."

"Instead you ran and tattled." Adam pointed to the last house on the street.

"I'm still not convinced Mom can't read minds."

"Why, bro? Something to hide? Park on the side."

Andrew avoided the question. "I see cameras on the doors. I assume you have this house fully secured."

"Yes. September wanted Harmony with her, so she nixed the hotel. There's even a toddler-sized playhouse in the backyard."

"Is Harmony old enough for one?" Andrew shut off the car and untangled Princess from her doggy car seat. "I wonder how Princess is with babies."

"FYI, you might be hired to guard the dog, but Harmony comes first if there's a dispute."

"Agreed. Niece over dog." Andrew checked the fenced backyard. "Hey, Princess, looks like you can run free." He let the dog loose in the fenced yard and entered the house through the kitchen door. Mom stood at the counter mixing something in a bowl. September sat in front of the highchair coaxing Harmony to eat pureed peas, judging from the greenish smears covering his niece's chin. Through the door, he could see one of the Hastings guards in the front room.

"Where's Jordan?"

"What, no 'Hello, Mom?'"

Andrew gave his mom a side hug and a kiss on the cheek. "If I'd said 'Hello, Mom' to you first, you would have scolded me for not checking on my client."

"My understanding is that your client is the one digging up the flower bed. But since you need to know, I told Jordan to lie down in my room. You better go rescue that garden before that mutt makes a bigger mess."

Tonie entered the kitchen. "I'll go get the dog. It'll give me a chance to practice my dog-grooming skills before someone wonders why I don't know the tail from the ears."

Mom used a teaspoon to point the way to Jordan. "Upstairs, second door on the left."

The door was half open, but Andrew tapped anyway. "May I come in?"

Jordan sat with her knees hugged to her chin in a chair by the window. She nodded.

"Do you mind if I leave the door open?"

A half smile graced her face. "Is it worse to be overheard or have people wonder why we closed the door?"

"If you're worried about eavesdroppers, I'm the only other person in the house who signs. No, I take that back. I've been teaching Harmony a few signs. But she can't interpret for anyone else and beyond *mama*, *dada*, and *milk*, she isn't much of a conversationalist. If you don't want to be overheard, we can sign."

"What, no cookie?" Jordan signed.

Andrew kept his hand in his pockets. "Not yet. I don't want to teach her any signs that'll get September upset with me. Did you meet my mom?"

"She took one look at me and told me to go take a nap. Do I look like I need one?"

Andrew drew circles around his eyes with his finger. "Not so much tired as exhausted in a mental or emotional way, I can see around the eyes. Mom is making her brownies—a cure-all."

"One of Grandma's cooks used to make me brownies all the time until the nutritionist told her to stop."

Andrew took a seat on the bed. He didn't want to bring up the scene they'd played in the trailer, and yet he found he was helpless to calm the tension in the room. "This house is fully secured. I wouldn't say your panic word anywhere in the house; it will set off security."

"The house is listening to us? Isn't that like Stu's bugs?"

"The system listens passively for panic words. It's listening for September's and Mom's words in addition to yours. Kind of like when you talk to your phone and have to use a certain phrase to get it to respond."

"That isn't very comforting." Jordan rolled her eyes. "Judging by the discussions I see on my social media, my phone is listening all the time. The week we shot *Princess Sam Sails the Seventh Sea*, I kept getting ads for yachts and life vests."

"The episode where you spent a third of the show in a rubber raft?"

"Yeah, so maybe I needed a life preserver."

Andrew signed "rolling on the floor with laughter," then spoke. "The only video in the house is on the entry doors and in Harmony's room. Most babies have no expectation of privacy. And anyone with the Hastings app can turn off the audio feeds for any room."

Jordan dropped one leg to the floor. "So you can turn off the audio in here?"

"I was going to when I came in, but it was already off. Mom must have wanted you to have your privacy without giving you the fine print."

"Thanks for letting me know. It's funny. I complain about my hotel room being bugged, and it is basically the same thing."

"Yes, only we tell you where and why. September chose the level of listening she wanted. If this were your place, you could choose the security level you want. We once put my sister in an undercover situation with so many cameras that only the bathroom had no visual, but it still had audio. She would play games and do things just to annoy us. Or she would talk to us at night when she couldn't sleep."

"That could come in handy." Jordan put the other leg down and turned to face him. "I know Tonie will be staying in the suite with me, but if I wanted to call you, could I?"

"How else am I supposed to learn the filming tricks of 1950s films?" Andrew hoped his smile conveyed the same message.

"This morning didn't—"

"Jordan, this morning when I woke up, I thought of you as a person with a great sense of humor and a gorgeous smile who happens to be an actor. This afternoon, the only part that has changed is that you are a very convincing actor with amazing empathy for others." He could have gone on but stopped.

"But I should have kicked Storm out and called HR or the Screen Actors Guild."

"I understand why you didn't. Publicity, backlash, and who knows? Neither of us could have guessed at the outcome of letting him in. We can both beat ourselves up for the other things we could have done. But we're still left with what happened."

Violence was rarely the answer, yet in this case, Andrew regretted not hitting the actor. "I'm determined to never leave you alone with him."

"Thanks. It could have been worse. What if Storm ..." Jordan shivered.

"I have a big question for you. Can you still work with me? The other day you trusted me to get you out of a threat area without any questions. Can you still let me in your personal space without freezing or second-guessing me?"

"As you said earlier, we're good. And I'm glad you were there. I think Stu and company would have left me alone with Storm, and that would have ended much worse."

Andrew nodded. After reading some Hollywood gossip blogs, he assumed the main reason Storm had taken this role was to clean up his reputation as a womanizer. "Usually, after an incident that doesn't end the way we hope, we brainstorm what to do to next time."

Jordan held up her hand. "There isn't going to be a next time. Storm is banned from my trailer and everywhere else for life. I do not need to feel degraded or degrade others to be a good actress."

"It probably won't help, but I think guys are wired differently—at least I am. I was shocked, but I don't feel degraded."

Jordan gave him a half smile. "Thanks. If you don't mind, I think I'm going to take that nap now. Don't let the house listen to me snoring."

Andrew laid his hand on top of Jordan's. "I suggest you don't snore, then. And definitely don't sleep talk about shoelaces."

Jordan looked at their hands and then at his face. "I won't."

Andrew shut the door as he left the room. On Sunday, he'd been ready to quit because he didn't think he should work for this client. Four days later, he wondered if he should quit because he wanted to kiss this client. Perhaps he needed a nap too.

"Cut! Great, September. Everyone take ten while we review film." Paul waved everyone off the set.

Jordan left her mark next to Storm and hurried around the extras to September. The last two days of filming had been grueling, and Paul's temper had risen with every take. As much as Jordan wanted to discuss her frustrations with Andrew, she refrained, allowing Tonie to take Princess to the dog park and staring at the phone late at night to avoid conversation. It would do no good for her bodyguard to know how disgusting she found Storm's touch on her bare back as they filmed the dance sequence over and over.

Adam stood at September's side, water bottles in each hand.

September handed an empty bottle to her fiancé, who was an extra in the scene. "I hope that is the last take. I want to be home for church tomorrow."

Jordan stretched a kink in her neck. "I will miss you when you go back."

"Me or Melanie Hastings's brownies? I haven't figured out how to compete with her brownies."

Adam wrapped an arm around September. "I'm sure we can come up with something better than Mom's baking."

September giggled, then abruptly stopped, her mouth a firm line. Jordan turned to see what had ruined the moment.

Storm. He looked from Adam to Jordan and then September. A momentary confusion crossed his face, quickly replaced by a fake smile. "September, I see you're working to get your squeaky-clean image back. I hear Hearthfire is the place to do that."

Adam's jaw tightened. September tapped his arm with a single finger, and he relaxed. "I'm not trying to be anything I'm not. I love to sing, and this show is a great debut for this song. Have you met my fiancé, Adam Hastings?"

Storm winced during the handshake. "Nice to meet you. You look a lot like this other guy hanging around the set."

Jordan ignored the pointed look Storm gave her. Adam didn't show such control. "You mean one of Jordan's bodyguards?"

"I think he guards the dog." Storm sneered as his gaze swept over Jordan's body.

She clenched her jaw and imagined she wore magic armor that repelled Storm. At least he'd kept his word and not doused himself with Thunder today.

Adam shifted, appearing taller and more muscular than a moment before. "One thing about my kid brother you should know. He has much more restraint than I do. I assume you have that trademark smirk insured?"

Storm made a poor attempt of looking down his nose at a man three inches taller. "If you are threatening me, I'll have you tossed off the lot."

"Since you can't tell whether you are being threatened, perhaps it would be best if you moved on." Adam inserted himself between Storm and Jordan.

Paul's high-pitched whistle ended the confrontation, giving Storm a reason to leave. Paul gave a second whistle. "Check your schedules for Monday's time and locations. We're done for today."

September touched Jordan's elbow. "Come stay with me for the weekend. I have a big house, and the bed beats anything the hotel has to offer."

"I'd love to. I probably should let Stu know."

"He won't make some of his bodyguards follow you, will he? They are not coming in my house."

Adam placed a hand on September's shoulder. "Let me talk with Stu. Meet you at the trailers."

"It'll take me awhile. Wardrobe sewed me into this dress." The designer hadn't wanted a zipper ruining his creation.

Andrew met Jordan at the trailer. "Stu says you're cleared to leave. Do you want to ride with Princess and me or in the SUV with the rest of the team?"

"I think I should stay with the dog." Jordan wasted no time in gathering her things.

Only a week ago, Andrew had been on this same highway heading north. Out of the corner of his eye, he checked his sleeping passenger. Jordan's phone rang. She didn't move. It rang again. She still didn't wake up.

Andrew's phone rang. He answered it through the car's hands-free system. A voice he recognized only from the movies came over the speakers. "Is this Andrew Hastings?"

"Yes."

"Where is my granddaughter?"

"She's sleeping."

"How do you know that?"

"She's right next to me." Only after the words left his mouth did he see the mental picture those words created.

"What?"

"We are in my car driving to Chicago. September Platt invited her down for the rest of the weekend."

"Jordan usually wakes up to my calls."

"Between you and me, I don't think she's been sleeping well."
I haven't.

"Will you have her call me when she wakes up? I'm staying in London a couple more days. Today's shooting was a disaster. The little boy who plays the grandson tossed his lunch all over. His mother didn't tell the director he was lactose intolerant and didn't intervene when someone handed him an ice cream cone."

Jordan squeaked and covered her mouth with both hands.

"Was that Jordan, or does the mutt have a new toy?"

Jordan shook her head vigorously.

"Um, Princess doesn't have any toys."

Jordan dropped her hands and glared at him. "Hi, Grandma."

"I wanted you to know I'm still in London. Anything new these past couple days? We haven't talked."

"Not much. Paul is stressed because we are behind schedule. One truck went to the wrong state. Apparently, the driver didn't know Wisconsin and Michigan aren't the same place."

Claire's laugh danced from the speakers. "I thought your generation wasn't supposed to get lost with GPS."

"Neither of us drive enough to know." Jordan yawned.

"You sound tired. Call me tomorrow."

"I will. Love you, Grandma."

"Love you too, bunny. Thanks for letting us use your phone, Andrew. Watch over her for me."

"I will." The call ended, and Jordan shifted in her seat. "Sorry you had to answer for me. I really was asleep. She must have gotten your number from Blake."

"Curious—why didn't you want to talk with her?" Andrew asked. "Don't answer that. It isn't any of my business." He needed to work on his client boundaries.

"It bothers you that we are friends, doesn't it?"

Andrew passed a slow-moving semi-truck. There wasn't a good answer. The truth was that every bit of his mind was rebelling against their friendship and what it meant for her safety. The nonlogical side of him wasn't bothered one bit. And that scared him. "Is this a trick question? I feel like I don't have a good answer. I'm your bodyguard. I'm not supposed to be your friend."

"You are Princess's bodyguard. You aren't supposed to be her friend."

"Yet a dog is man's best friend, so you see my problem." Andrew followed Adam and September's vehicle off at an exit.

"No, I can't say I do."

With nothing to say to her response, they drove in silence to the gated community where September lived.

The baby, the dog, the luggage, and the diaper bags required several trips into the house to unload. Andrew stifled a laugh at the realization that the baby and dog each required as much stuff as the adult humans combined.

September and Harmony disappeared upstairs, leaving everyone else standing in the kitchen.

Adam helped himself to a glass of water. "I'm going to stay here for a couple hours. Mom, can you get a ride with Andrew?"

"Sure. Andrew, would you mind stopping by Alex's? I found the cutest cheese T-shirt in a baby boutique. Little Clay doesn't get spoiled as often as the triplets do."

All five of his "niblings," a term he'd learned from the internet for nieces and nephews, were plenty spoiled in his opinion—not that he would ever tell his mother.

"No problem."

"Jordan, come with September to the house tomorrow for Sunday dinner. Abbie can't make it, so we will have plenty of room."

"I wouldn't want to impose."

Adam laughed. "Not possible. Mom is happy only when the house is full of noise. There's no way you can make enough noise to even begin to replace two adults, three babies, and a chauffeur plus whatever bodyguard gets driveway duty."

"Well, if you're sure…"

Mom beamed. "Positive. Are you allergic to any foods?"

Jordan shook her head.

Andrew hustled his mother out with only the briefest of goodbyes, then waited until September's house was in his rearview mirror. "Mom, Jordan is a client. Why are you asking her to the house?"

"You mean other than it would be rude to make her stay at September's alone with her dog tomorrow afternoon? I thought I raised you with some semblance of manners."

"I understand, but she is a client, and we rarely have clients to the house. The whole personal-boundaries lecture comes to mind here." Andrew's weak defense sounded worse out loud.

"Are you having issues with boundaries regarding Miss Lee?" His mother stared at him as he merged back on to the freeway.

"Things are more complicated with her. I'm spending more one-on-one time with her than I do with other clients. I'm glad Tonie came as we aren't talking on the phone as much, which is helping."

"Then there was the kiss."

"How do you know about that?" Andrew racked his brain for a way the news could have reached her.

"I'm a mom. It is my job to know things. I'm concerned it might have affected your working relationship."

"In what way?"

"You can't play that game with me. I'm not going to give you the answer I'm looking for." Not the mom-lecture voice.

"So the question is, am I having boundary issues? Yes, I am. But I think with Tonie on duty, we are getting back to a more normal bodyguard/principal relationship. Jordan is used to relying on Mr. Blake as almost a father figure." No sense mentioning how Mr. Blake had basically gone all protective dad on him.

"I know how much you want to be your own person and not follow in your siblings' footsteps. Remember when you insisted on being called Drew?"

He took the exit for Alex and Kimberly's condo. "I thought it would make it so my name wouldn't be AdamAlanAlexAbbieAndrew, and all it changed was I became AdamAlanAlexAbbieAndrewImeanDrew."

"I'm sorry. At the time, I thought it was cute. I still do. But back to my point. Sometimes you've made choices with the only purpose being to not be like your siblings. I know most of them have taken the rule not to be emotionally involved with a client as a guideline. And to a certain extent, they were all correct. Although I still can't believe how Alex's fake marriage turned out. Anyway, don't make Adam's mistake. He shouldn't have walked away. In the end, some rules were meant to be broken."

Andrew pulled into Alex's condo as Alex and Kimberly were pulling out. They rolled down their windows. The short exchange had his mother switching cars and Andrew going home alone.

HARMONY STUFFED A PINK GIRAFFE in her mouth and kicked her feet against the seat. Jordan had never ridden in a back seat with a baby and found the spectacle entertaining.

September turned and looked over her shoulder. "Don't let her fall asleep on the ride to Grandma's. She gets cranky if we wake her up."

"You refer to Mrs. Hastings as Grandma?"

September gazed adoringly at Adam, who drove. "Even though it isn't official, it seemed like the best way to teach her since by the time she is talking, Adam and I'll be married and he will legally be her dad."

"Mom thinks she already calls her GeGe." Adam turned into an eighties-era subdivision.

"She calls Adam A-da. I'm working on getting the first *D* in there."

Jordan didn't ask about Harmony's birth father. His conviction for attempted double homicide had been all over the papers. By the time he got out of prison, Harmony would be in college.

Adam pulled into the driveway. "Here we are—the weekly Sunday dinner."

The front door opened, and a man who could only be the patriarch of the family came out. He reached the passenger door next to Harmony before Adam and September. "There's Grandpa's little angel."

Melanie Hastings stood on the front porch. "Never mind Jethro. He is jealous I had Harmony all to myself the past couple days. Like he didn't have four grandsons he could have visited."

Jethro carted Harmony into the house. "But this is my only granddaughter."

"Come on in, Jordan. We are very informal around here. Where's Princess?"

"I left her at September's. There is a nice fenced yard there." Jordan looked around the front room. Andrew had told her his home was one of the securest in the country because they kept using it to test different security systems, but there wasn't a camera she could see.

Melanie ushered the group through the house. "Come out on the back porch. The boys are back there. This morning's rain dried up, and today may be the last good Sunday we get. The last one in September usually is."

Andrew stood near the barbecue with the two Hastings brothers Jordan hadn't met. The one with the baby in his arms had to be Alex. Adam joined them. All four were scrutinizing the meat.

"They're formidable, aren't they?" said a brunette by her elbow. "I'm Kimberly, Alex's wife. The first time I saw them all together I nearly choked, but muscles always impress me. And those Hastings blue eyes? September needs to write a song about them."

"Are you kidding? Every woman in the country would be after Adam. I'm not sharing." September joined them, holding a lemonade.

Kimberly tapped her chin. "It would do wonders for Alan's and Andrew's dating lives. Could you imagine?"

"I imagine Elle not being happy. She needs more time for Alan to see what's in front of him." September sipped her drink. "Which leaves Andrew, and I can't write only about his eyes. Nothing against Adam, but Andrew got the best hair of the group."

Jordan silently agreed. Andrew's slightly darker wavy hair made her fingers itch. It didn't help that the object of their conversation was walking toward them, his blue eyes on her.

"Hey, I see you met Kimberly. Do you want to meet my other brothers?"

Jordan followed him across the patio.

"This big guy with the baby is Alex; the short one is Alan."

"Hey, I'm only shorter by a half inch. Nice to meet you, Jordan." Alan extended a hand. Alex nodded.

"We were just discussing y—" started Alan.

"Alan, not now." Andrew tried to step between Alan and Jordan.

Alex put a hand on Andrew's shoulder. The wordless-man-communication thing happened, and Alex won. "To be specific, we were discussing your security. One of our clients is hosting a ribbon cutting and gala for a children's cancer ward this week. Andrew's planned the security for it, and we feel it would be best if he were there. Ben, who is one of our team leaders, would take over in Wisconsin with your security. With Tonie on your detail, we feel they'll do a great job."

Andrew shrugged off his brother's hand. "My plan is straightforward. They don't need me."

"I volunteered to go up, but September is performing at the gala," said Adam.

Jordan tipped her chin and studied the four brothers. "Andrew, did you plan this before I disrupted your schedule?"

"Yes."

"I assume your client trusts your expertise. Theirs is a prior commitment. If you feel Ben and Tonie can see to my security, then you should be here. You trust Ben, don't you?"

"Definitely. He wouldn't be a team leader if we didn't," answered Andrew.

Jordan used a smile she knew to be convincing. "Then you're leaving me in good hands. I understand that I disrupted your schedule."

Andrew narrowed his eyes but didn't argue.

Adam stepped forward. "If you'd like, I can come up and stay until Thursday, since the gala is Friday."

Tempting. She glanced to where September and Kimberly spoke with Jethro. September needed her fiancé more than Jordan did Andrew. "Thank you for the offer, but I'm sure Ben will be fine."

Andrew studied her too closely, his brow wrinkling as he opened his mouth, then closed it.

Jordan tossed all the brothers a smile. "I will go join the girls while you guys finish the burgers."

She turned to discover the women no longer congregating. September and Jethro were deep in conversation, and Melanie and Kimberly, nowhere to be seen, must be in the house. Determined to leave, Jordan headed in the direction of a large wooden play yard complete with a fort on top.

Andrew caught up with her as she circled the slide. "Tell me how you really feel about this week's change in plans."

"Did your father build this, or was it a kit?" Jordan spun around a fireman's pole.

Andrew blocked her path, his arms crossed. "You put on your acting face back there. Why?"

Moving around Andrew, Jordan used the teeter-totter as a balance beam. "With what you've told me about your family, I'm surprised no one was killed out here." When she reached the point when the teeter-totter should rebalance and send her downhill, it didn't. Jordan looked over her shoulder to find Andrew standing on the seat end, arms crossed, an eyebrow raised. He was cute when persistent. Jordan jumped down and crossed to the swing. As soon as she sat down, she knew she'd chosen wrongly. Pushing off, she got in two good pumps, hoping a moving target was better than a sitting one. One more pump and she could jump clear. Strong arms wrapped around her waist, stopping her at the highest point of her backswing.

"Jordan." Andrew's voice vibrated through her like a guard-dog's growl.

"Let me go. Your entire family is staring."

"Only if you answer my questions."

"Fine."

Andrew released her. At the top of the arc, Jordan jumped. The ladder to the fort was only feet away. She made it to the first rung when Andrew came behind her, trapping her. "You realize if you go up, there isn't an easy way down as the ropes on the other side are missing?"

Jordan stepped back down and turned to face him. Andrew leaned his arm overhead on the entrance to the fort. "Mom's brother designed this. Now, you owe me an answer."

"Fine. No, I'm not happy. I was getting used to you, and I don't just spill my thoughts to anyone, and it's super annoying when you say I'm acting when I'm dealing with the situation. It isn't like I really have a choice, is it?" The words rushed out in one long breath.

"There are always choices. I could rearrange things. Any of my brothers could execute my plans for the gala."

"But your other client wouldn't be happy, and your brothers might miss a detail and you would spend all week worrying about it." Jordan crossed her arms.

"And all week I will wonder how you are really doing and if I need to punch Storm in the face." His voice lowered.

"Probably should on Wednesday. We film our first kiss. Assuming Paul adheres to the agreed intimacy guidelines, it should be fine. But that doesn't mean Storm won't be a jerk about it."

"Will you call me?"

Jordan met his eyes. "You mean I can?"

"Text me first. We may need to set up a time. And give me ten minutes to answer the text." Andrew pushed back from the fort, giving her more room.

Jordan didn't bother holding back the smile. "I'd like that."

Andrew held out his hand. "Let's go get some burgers before my brothers eat them all."

As busy as his week was, Andrew found too much time to think about Jordan. The brief calls were not enough to keep him from wondering if Storm was acting like a gentleman, a feat that would require most of the man's acting skills, or if Ben and Tonie were being vigilant.

Jordan had been elated that Wednesday's kissing scene required only one take and that Storm hadn't worn Thunder. Andrew wasn't sure which one Jordan was happiest about. Ben reported that one note had been left in the trailer but Tonie had intercepted it. The computer-written note had been sent to Blake for the collection. No one bothered to let Stu know about it.

Somehow Andrew made it to Friday. So far, the ribbon cutting was without incident. The hour before the start of the gala had the entire Hastings team working to run things safely, smoothly, and invisibly.

The gala had more moving parts than most events—celebrities with their own protection details, local politicians with only a month left to impress voters, and philanthropists, some famous, others not, milling about. Add in the caterers, event staff, and local and national media outlets and it all totaled a mind-blowing amount of people to watch. Most of the Chicago-area security agencies worked and played well together on events like this. Only three of the attendees were under active threat alerts. The attendance of the mayor meant the police were there, and two federal judges brought the US Marshals, both of which were less likely to follow a civilian command.

Elle entered the command room. "The caterer is upset. She added three people to her staff today, but they didn't have background clearances. Alex won't let them in. She threatened to quit, and I told her to double-check her contract. Alan is running backgrounds now."

"It always happens. You think they'd know by now to have extra staff on hand. Any other glitches?"

"No, but did you see the background check on the councilman? No way is he getting my vote."

Andrew laughed. "He isn't the only one. You'd better get changed and back out there. Alex will want you near the red carpet."

Elle took a dress bag from over a chair. "It isn't fair that the only time I get to wear gorgeous clothes is at work. I hope I don't need to chase anyone down in this little black dress. I'd like to use it on a date someday. I'll be back in ten."

Andrew's phone vibrated. He expected it to be the Hastings app. It was Jordan.

—Hard day. Talk?

Gala starts in 45 min. I can for about 2 minutes or after 1 a.m.

—Okay. We can talk in the morning. Hope all goes well.

Thanks

Andrew stared at his phone. Jordan knew the schedule for today. His thumb hovered over the call button. Alan's voice boomed in his ear. "One of the detained caterers has two outstanding warrants, one gun-related. Is CPD on-site?"

Andrew checked the monitors. "Not yet. Alex, are they still in holding?"

"Yes. Let me guess—the blond guy? He's pacing like a caged tiger."

"I'm putting in a call to the police," said Alan. "Let me know if he gets too antsy. The female has worked with us before. She's free to work with the caterer."

"I'll get her out here now," said Alex.

Elle came back into the room. "I'd be better off in flats, but this is the best dress yet."

Andrew turned from his computer screens. "Abbie picked it out. She's missed being in the business. I believe the pockets are custom."

"Tell her thanks and to ditch the heels next time."

Andrew laughed. "You're supposed to blend in at the end of the red carpet." He snuck another look at his phone.

"Is something wrong?"

"It's Jordan. She texted and asked for a phone call. I just can't right now."

Elle fixed her earpiece. "When I come back to change after the red carpet, I'll watch the monitors for you and give you a five- or ten-minute break. Test my comm, will you?"

Andrew leaned close to the speaker. "Elle looks like a movie star."

A grumble came over the line. Elle and Andrew exchanged grins. Poor Alan, back at the office. Elle waved and left. A moment later, she appeared on the monitor of the lobby camera.

Alex's voice came over the comms. "The police escorted both new hires off in handcuffs."

"Both?" Andrew and Alan asked in unison.

"Second guy tried to make a break for it and threw a punch at the officer. Any idea who he was, Alan?"

"None. Other than the name he gave us is an alias. Looks like the Ogilvies' car is one minute out. You guys ready down there?" Alan asked.

Andrew broadcast onto all the communication devices. "First car is here."

The next hour flew by. One aggressive photographer and a protester were easily taken care of. The only surprises came from his own family. Abbie and Preston arrived with Preston's parents. Abbie, Preston, and his mother carried the triplets in their arms. September brought Harmony. All four children left with their nannies and bodyguards after the red carpet. Abbie borrowed Elle's comm to apologize and claimed it was a last-minute change.

No one believed her. Nothing with the triplets was last minute. September had put in her security plan that Harmony's attendance was a possibility.

Elle returned to the operations room. "Please let me get off my feet for a few minutes." She plopped into the chair next to Andrew. "These shoes look so much nicer than they feel."

"We are fifteen minutes out from September's first song. Deidre is with her. Mrs. Crawford may need a female guard. She isn't feeling well. We took Tonie off her team. Remind Alan to fix that."

"Mr. Crawford knows she's expecting?" As with many of their longtime clients, the Hastings Security bodyguards knew a fair amount of secrets by observation. Morning sickness wasn't easy to hide. Elle hadn't worked much with the Crawford's, but she loved Mandy Crawford's down to earth view of things.

"Her husband knew before we did, but they don't want to make a public announcement."

"Go make your phone call. I'll change and let the Crawford's detail know I am available." Elle rubbed her feet.

"I shouldn't leave."

"You've looked at your phone twice since I came in, and everything security related from the app is on your laptop. Go make the call."

Andrew picked up his phone.

"Knock before you come back in. I'm going to change back into my suit."

Andrew stood outside the door since it didn't lock and dialed Jordan's number. It rang several times before going to voicemail.

According to Blake's app, Jordan's phone was at the hotel. Andrew called it again.

Straight to voicemail.

Andrew left a message. "Hi, I'll call again later."

It wasn't much, but if she happened to play her messages around anyone else, it would be enough.

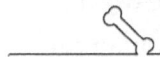

Princess tried to lick Jordan's face. Arching her neck, Jordan escaped the doggy affection. "I don't need kisses. Kisses aren't love. Right now I just need snuggles." Jordan settled on the center of the bed. Princess curled up next to her, laying her head on Jordan's lap. As Jordan scratched behind the dog's ears, Princess stretched to expose the underside of her chin.

"You're a little beggar, aren't you?" Jordan flipped on the TV and surfed to the old-movies channel. The feature wasn't one of her grandmother's, but it included an actor Grandma always said was one of the good guys. The noise would cover any sound she and Princess made. Tonie wasn't nosey or anything, but she wasn't BFF material, and there wasn't anyone else in the hotel she could talk to. If word got back to Paul about how much she detested her leading man, it would not be good. Reggie might roll her eyes in public over Storm, but she followed all his fan groups in private. And it was no secret that Kittie had a crush on Storm, as did most of the female and a few male crew members.

Her phone rang. Andrew. The time showed below his name. He must have gotten away for a few moments. If she answered, she would cry, and then he might be distracted. There were too many people counting on him tonight. She let the call go to voicemail.

"Do you think he'll believe I went out?"

Princess turned her head, expecting to have her other ear scratched.

Jordan turned up the volume, glad this was not a romance movie. Her phone rang again. She swiped at the icon, sending Andrew's call to voicemail again.

The first guests to leave were the Crawfords, who exited via the service door. Other couples and VIPs filtered out, and soon only security and custodial staff remained in the building. Andrew gave orders to the tech crew to pull the cameras and feeds. Elle came into the operations room and put the communications links she had gathered from the various details into their cases.

Andrew checked his text messages.

"Did she answer?"

"No. Tonie said she is in her room and there haven't been any security incidents."

"What are you going to do?"

"Call her tomorrow like she asked?"

"Are you asking me if that's the correct answer?"

Andrew unplugged his laptop from the monitors. "Maybe?"

"Sorry. You are asking the wrong person. I don't know her well enough to give you any advice. I can finish here with the equipment, and you can take off early and call her."

"I shouldn't leave you alone in the building."

Elle tapped her headset. "Alex, are you still in the building?"

"Yes."

"Andrew is going to take off. Will you stay until things are closed up? I don't want him in trouble with Alan."

Alex's laugh came across the comms. "We can't have that."

"I can hear you." Alan growled.

"O, wise, omnipresent brother. Have no fear. We won't leave Elle alone," teased Alex.

"Of course you wouldn't. There is no 'one' in team, and Hastings is always a team." Alan didn't sound as perturbed as he had earlier. "Andrew, I've put you on the schedule to replace Ben on Jordan's detail Sunday afternoon."

"Thanks." Andrew put his personal items in his backpack.

Elle held out her hand. "Comms?"

Andrew pulled his earpiece out and handed it to Elle, then grabbed it back and spoke into the mic. "Thanks, Elle, you're the best."

Elle shook her head and waved him out of the room.

11:32. Too late to call. Andrew texted as he walked down the hall. **Just got off work. Call me if you want to talk.**

The phone rang as he pulled into his apartment complex. He parked as he answered. "Hey, sorry it is so late, but I'm glad you called."

"You won't be in a moment." Jordan's voice hiccupped. Andrew wasn't sure if it was the connection or her.

"Why not?" Andrew held the phone to his ear as he exited the car.

"Storm was wearing a button cam that day. He ... he says if I don't go to brunch with him, he'll post the video of the kiss."

Andrew tripped on the curb. "When?"

"I'm not sure. Paul made a schedule change, and we're shooting tomorrow out at the mansion. Sunday at the earliest."

The sounds coming over the phone were sobs, not static.

"What time are you leaving for tomorrow's shoot?" Andrew opened his door and turned the lights on.

"Five a.m. Paul wants to try the sunrise scenes, and tomorrow's weather looks good."

"I can be there at 4:30." In his bedroom, Andrew started pulling out the clothes he would need for another week.

"It won't do any good. Princess isn't allowed on location, so you won't be allowed. Storm isn't likely to try anything on set after today anyway." Jordan's sobs faded as her voice grew louder.

"Jordan? What happened today?" Andrew sat on the end of his bed.

"We reshot the first kiss."

"But you did that on Wednesday." It had been their longest call of the week.

"The file got corrupted or something. We had to do three takes. And Maria and Reggie threatened to report Storm to the SAG."

"Maria?"

"She's my makeup artist." Jordan took a deep breath. Andrew knew it the moment she pulled out her actress self and started plowing through without tears. "I asked that she be on set, mostly because there are only a couple of females among the crew. I knew she would speak up if Storm tried to push things on set. Since it's only a kiss, I don't need a SAG intimacy coordinator or anything, but as you know, even a kiss can get out of hand. And Storm is pretty annoyed with how G-rated our first kiss was."

"What happened?"

"It took three takes today. I don't want to detail them. Paul was pretty ticked after the second, and that had nothing to do with Maria yelling "Cut!" and getting between us and the camera. Fortunately, Paul made Storm stick to the script. But he hinted that he might modify the wedding kiss if Storm would behave."

"Can they do that?" Andrew hastily folded his shirts.

"Within reason. This is a Hearthfire show, but the script calls for a longer kiss. No tongue, but, as you know, it can still be fairly uncomfortable without."

"Are you sure Storm had a camera?"

"He showed me the footage. I look like a—" Jordan started sobbing again.

"I'll be up there before you leave for the mansion."

"No. You've worked overtime all week. I want you to sleep. Then you can drive up here safely. Please promise me you will."

Andrew closed his eyes. The pull to hop in his car was almost as strong as the pull to abide by her wishes. "I won't leave until I've slept."

"At least five hours of sleep. I see your loophole." There was a hint of a smile in her voice.

"You know me too well."

"You're my bodyguard. Good night. Get some sleep. And thank you for calling. I think I can sleep now."

"Good night. Sleep well."

"Drive safe."

The line went dead. Andrew stared at the dark screen as if it could teleport his thoughts, or even himself, to her.

"Cut! And lunch break!"

Jordan shook out her arms.

Reggie did likewise. "Why did we agree to another archery scene?"

"We forgot how fatiguing it is to stand still while they film and we never get to shoot."

"Just once I want to hit a target or something. It would be cool to see if we could have really shot the grappling hook up the side of the ship last year." Jordan handed her bow over to the property's manager.

"What are we supposed to be shooting this time, anyway?" asked Reggie.

"Wolves."

"You are kidding me, right?" Reggie handed her quiver of arrows to Kittie.

"You sat in the same read-through I did, didn't you? The wolves are threatening the town's Christmas festival in our home country."

"I thought we killed all of them off in season one."

"Me too. But this time we need help."

Reggie burst into laughter. "Oh, this is the opening sequence, isn't it? I wasn't paying too much attention to the notes as there wasn't any dialogue."

Jordan shook her head. "Thinking about your next movie?"

"Yes, I'm so excited. We start shooting in January!"

"For what?"

"Can't tell you. But I will as soon as the press release is out. Let's go get lunch before Paul calls us back for the next scene." Reggie gave a low whistle. "It looks like someone is waiting for you."

Jordan's steps slowed. Andrew conversed with Stu over near the buffet table. Her heart sped up before her feet did. She stopped at the table for a sandwich and sliced cucumbers.

"Mr. Andrew, you made good time."

"The sun rose nearly six hours ago. Stu gave me permission to stick around." He smiled an easy smile, and Jordan's world brightened.

"We only have one more sequence. Paul is shooting the opening credits. I'm hunting down a wolf in the forest using day for night. He likes how the sun is filtering through the trees and says it's perfect for the full moon he envisions. He'd like snow, but ..." Jordan shrugged. At least he wasn't using the fake stuff.

"He may get snow in another three weeks. Not uncommon for kids to trick-or-treat in snow boots and coats." Andrew picked up a sandwich.

"Paul is hoping to make the Christmas wedding perfect. That is why the last scene in the film is actually scheduled to be shot last. If we get snow earlier, he will move things around."

"Jordan, I've been looking for you." Storm's voice caused her to stiffen. "I hope you have an answer for our brunch tomorrow."

Jordan counted to three before she turned around. "May I choose the place?"

"My cook will make it for us at my cottage. Would ten work?"

Jordan turned to Stu. "Can you accompany me tomorrow?"

"Certainly, Miss Lee."

"He can't come." Storm stuck out his chin, reminding Jordan of the five-year-old she'd worked with earlier that year.

"Miss Lee had an attack on her life two weeks ago. Hearthfire is committed to her safety. She doesn't go anywhere without authorized security." Stu crossed his arms.

"But I'm in the cast."

"And it requires a thirty-five-mile drive from Miss Lee's hotel."

Storm crossed his arms and glared at Andrew. "But she left with him last weekend."

"Mr. Andrew is a member of Hastings Security, as is Mr. Adam, who was with them, and four other personal-security personnel as they escorted Miss Platt and Miss Lee to Chicago for the weekend. Miss Lee's security was taken care of." Stu stared the actor down.

"Well then, you escort her or send Rod."

"I don't have the personnel. But I'll make sure she has security." Stu turned to Andrew. "Mr. Andrew, as Storm's brunch is Sunday and most of my crew has the day off, I wonder if I could hire you for the morning?"

"I can arrange that."

Joy bubbled up in Jordan. Stu and Andrew had rescued her. Storm glared at her, then left.

Kittie ran over to the table. "Miss Lee, the director wants you back up on the hill at the top of the hour."

"Thanks, Kittie." Jordan checked the watch wardrobe had given her. "Yikes! I have two minutes. Bye!"

Andrew spent the rest of the afternoon with Stu, getting a feel for the location. "This place is massive. It makes my sister's place seem small."

"The original owner wanted a Scottish castle. Although I think he modeled his home after a famous German one. One of my concerns is we only have partial floor plans and the place is rumored to have secret passages. I've cautioned Miss Lee to stay in sight." Stu led Andrew through the main hall. "I found an entrance to one over by the fireplace."

"Have there been any threats this week?" asked Andrew, curious if Stu had shared any information with Ben.

"None that Miss Lee saw, but there was a photo of her father taped to her door. I sent it to Blake."

Andrew nodded. Mr. Blake hadn't mentioned anything. He would check with him later.

"And this is the ballroom. Paul contracted the place because of this room."

"This room is out of a fairy tale." Andrew turned slowly, taking in the gilded wood, mirrors, and chandeliers. Hidden balconies and nooks abounded. The ballroom would be a nightmare to properly secure for a real event.

Stu's radio beeped. He took the message through his earpiece. "They are finished. Will you take Miss Lee back to town? We are leaving her trailer here. I put her in the same car as Paul, but it will be better if he can't vent on any of the cast if something else went wrong."

"No problem." Andrew followed Stu out of the house. The cast and crew worked to put away any props and equipment, and Stu left in the direction of the trailers. Andrew watched as the trailers were filled and locked and the cars and SUVs began to leave. Andrew searched for Jordan and found her exiting her trailer in jeans and a sweatshirt. "Hey, Stu said I could ride back with you."

"Do you mind?"

"Not at all. You are the only person on set besides Maria who won't care if I close my eyes and take a nap instead of talking."

Andrew showed her to his car, one of only three left in the driveway.

"Looks like most of the cast has gone. I didn't think I took that long."

Andrew started his car and eased it onto the one-lane road. "I didn't think you did either. Try to get some sleep. And I'll keep it under the speed limit."

Jordan leaned back and closed her eyes. "Everyone wants to go out and eat tonight at some restaurant. Will you come with me?"

"As a bodyguard or friend?"

"Stu's approved the place, so you can come as a friend."

"I'd like that."

Jordan was asleep within seconds, and Andrew's world felt right again.

20

THE THIRD WEEK IN GREEN Bay started off with Storm postponing their brunch. Monday's and Tuesday's filming couldn't have gone better as the cast and crew started to meld. Jordan's only complaint was that after Ben left, she hadn't seen Andrew as much as she would have liked. Wednesday didn't go smoothly as rain ruined the outdoor scenes. Instead, Jordan and Storm filmed a couple of dialogue scenes. There were multiple takes as Storm wore Thunder and Jordan kept gagging.

Thursday's filming wrapped up early, and there would be no filming Friday, mostly because the entire crew and most of the cast planned to go to the Thursday-night Packer's football game.

Spirits were high as they emptied the lot. Andrew and Tonie waited with Princess at the trailer. "You're early."

Jordan bent down to scratch Princess behind the ears. "Another one of those miracle days where we got almost everything on the first take. I've never been much for football, but bless the Packers and all the Cheeseheads."

Tonie and Andrew laughed.

"I'm glad the games are good for something. I shopped for dog food this morning, and the town has gone crazy," said Tonie.

"They're playing well this year, and it isn't supposed to be freezing tonight. Another week or so and they risk having their games in the snow. The locals will still turn out, but you Californians might not take it so well." Andrew laughed.

Jordan slipped into the bedroom and changed into her own clothes. She exited pulling a sweatshirt over her head. "We aren't as big of wimps as you think we are."

"You also don't have stadiums where they heat the football field to keep the ground from freezing." Tonie put Princess on her leash. "I'm glad you aren't going. I'm a basketball girl, and even baseball. Never been a fan freezing my tail off to watch men tackle each other. I had enough of watching my brothers do that. I respect the skills and all, but I want to be warm."

Stu knocked on the trailer door. "Hastings, do you have anyone else up here?"

"Ben came up with a detail today to set up Claire Lee's house."

"One of my guys just puked his guts out, so I'm down some security. Since no one but Miss Lee and a couple of staffers will be at the hotel tonight, can you guys take over her detail? That gives me a man to put here on the lot."

"Sure. If Jordan is fine with the change."

"May we go to the dog park?" Princess's ears perked up at Jordan's request.

Stu stopped on his way out. "I don't see a problem with that."

As soon as the door shut, Tonie pulled out her phone. "I'll see if Ben is still here. The tech team Blake hired to set up Claire Lee's condo should be done by now." She walked to the front of the trailer.

"Looks like you're stuck with me again." Jordan sat down on the couch and tied her tennis shoes.

Andrew crossed his arms and suppressed a smile. "Good. Maybe I can beat you in that game of checkers you promised me."

"Maybe I can convince you to get me more of those cheese curds."

Tonie came back. "They'll drop Ben off at the hotel. He has his go-bag."

Jordan studied the way Tonie had said Ben. Could they be a couple?

The wind swirled the fallen leaves around the base of the trees in the dog park. Princess played a rousing game of hide the ball from herself before collapsing at Jordan's feet. "Ready to go have dinner?"

Tonie strapped Princess into her car seat. "Drop me off at the hotel before you grab dinner. Princess and fast food don't belong in a car together."

"Do you want us to pick you anything up?" asked Jordan.

"Ben can order for me."

At the hotel, Ben traded places with Tonie in the car. He sat quietly as he had the week before. Silent and observant. Jordan longed to make him smile. As they waited for their meals at the drive-up, she asked her phone to tell them cheese jokes, hoping to lighten the mood.

The syncopated computer voice asked. "What do you call cheese that isn't yours?"

One corner of Ben's mouth raised. "Nacho cheese. You know I'm Wisconsin born and raised. There isn't a cheese joke I haven't heard."

A worker handed Andrew the bags of food.

"That's disappointing. Although all the ones I found don't seem that funny." Jordan swiped through her phone, looking for more.

"My favorite is terrible. When should you keep an eye on your cheese?" asked Ben.

"When you have mice?" asked Jordan.

"When it's up to no Gouda," answered Andrew as he pulled into the hotel lot.

Jordan pressed her hand to her forehead. "These are bad."

Andrew and Ben accompanied her to the elevator.

"When I was six, my sister bought me a shirt that said, 'I'm doing great, but I could be cheddar.' I wore it for my first-grade picture day. I don't know that my mother ever forgave me," said Ben.

They laughed all the way down the hall. At her door, shifting her food bag to one hand, Jordan pulled out her phone and waved it in front of the card reader. The light turned green, and she opened the door. Ben entered first and started a clockwise search of the room. Andrew followed with the drinks and a bag of food.

Princess didn't bound over to her. She must be out with Tonie.

Jordan turned the corner into the kitchenette to set the takeout bag down.

"Aglet!"

Andrew dropped his bag and scooped Jordan up, the sight of the prone bodies of Tonie and Princess registering in his mind as he rushed out of the room. He didn't have to tell Ben what to do. Andrew hesitated, deciding between the stairs and the elevator, then hit the down arrow to see if the elevator was still there. The door opened, and Andrew stepped inside, then shut the door and set Jordan down.

"Jordan, I need you to start acting. You will walk out of this elevator and to my car like nothing happened. Once inside, you can cry all you want. Okay?"

Jordan nodded. The elevator pinged as it stopped at the first floor. Andrew took Jordan by the hand and crossed the lobby. Once in the car, he locked the doors and hit a button on his console, calling Hastings dispatch. Whoever worked the switchboard didn't get to finish their greeting. "Patch me into Ben's phone."

"Connected."

"Ben?"

"Call 911. Suite is clear. There's an open bottle of water. I suspect ketamine. I wouldn't have let you both in the suite, but the app showed Tonie was in there, and I assumed..."

"As did I," said Andrew.

"911. What is your emergency?" Another voice joined the conversation.

Andrew put his phone on mute and listened as Ben requested an ambulance and a veterinarian.

Jordan grabbed his hand. Ben calmly informed the 911 operator of Tonie's condition including pulse rate. Both Princess and Tonie were breathing without problem. Andrew switched the call to his earpiece.

"Why did you do that?"

"Because you're squeezing my hand harder each moment, and they're at the point where 911 is keeping Ben on the line by repeating questions."

Jordan relaxed her death grip. "What's going on?"

"From what Ben is saying, it looks like someone may have put a drug in a water bottle. Help is on the way. If Ben can take care of this without having the police question you, he will. We were only in the room for a few seconds." He reached for Jordan's hand.

She leaned over and leaned into his chest. "Why me? Why me?"

Andrew had no answers.

Sirens wailed in the distance as three police cars and an ambulance pulled into the drop-off in front of the hotel. "Ben, they're here. Keep broadcasting."

Jordan put her hand over his. "Don't shut me out. I want to listen." She had put on her strong voice.

Andrew changed the audio back to the speakers. They sat in silence as they listened to Ben rehearse the incident to the officer.

"Who else was with you? And don't tell me no one. You have four dinners here."

"Jordan Lee and Andrew Hastings, her bodyguard. He evacuated her. They are nearby if you want to question them."

"Miss Lee again?"

"Yes, sir."

"I'll want to question her, but it can wait until after we test the water and get Miss ... ? What did you say her name was?"

"Tonie Day."

"Miss Day and the dog medical treatment. I'll send the dog to the vet our K-9 unit uses. They're the best in town."

Andrew and Jordan watched the paramedics exit the building with Tonie on a gurney. An officer carried Princess to a patrol car.

The officer's voice continued over the speakers. "I will seal this room as a crime scene. Please apologize to Miss Lee for any inconvenience and find her someplace safer than this hotel. What are you going to do now?"

There was a pause before Ben answered. "It's my duty to check on Miss Lee. Then I will go to the hospital to keep a watch on Tonie."

"I'll make sure they find you to tell you the status of the dog. Here's my number."

"Thanks, Officer."

"Tell Miss Lee her dog is in good hands and I'll talk with her later."

"Will do."

Andrew pulled out of the lot by the far exit before the officer or Ben could leave the building.

"Where are we going?"

"September's." Andrew unmuted his phone. "Dispatch, send a copy of the tape and an incident report to Mr. Blake. If you can reach him, I'd like to talk with him ASAP. Also, contact Stu with Hearthfire security and give him an abbreviated report. I'm taking Miss Lee to September's. Do not disclose the location to Hearthfire."

"Anything else, Mr. Andrew?"

"Yes. Ben came up with the tech team to set up Claire Lee's condo. The rest of the team is probably only an hour or so out.

Turn them around and send me a full detail."

"I have Mr. Blake on the line."

"Hello, Mr. Blake, it's Andrew."

"Jordan?"

"I'm here. I'm unharmed. I just don't understand."

"Neither do I, darling. Andrew, are you keeping her safe?"

"Yes, sir. We are moving to a safe house now."

"I'll review what you've sent me and call you back soon."

Andrew pulled into the driveway of September's home and opened the garage door via the Hastings app.

"Dispatch, good job tonight. Keep me updated." Andrew turned off the car and phone. "Stay in the car while I make sure the house is clear."

No offense to the Hastings app or its creators, but both he and Ben had relied on it to assume the hotel suite was clear since it showed Tonie in the suite. The only thing out of place in the safe house was Harmony's missing binky, in the center of the crib, which explained why September hadn't been able to find it in the diaper bag.

He returned to the car and opened Jordan's door. She didn't move. Andrew crouched down to be at eye level with her. "Jordan, come inside."

She turned to face him, tears pooling in her eyes. "If it was in the water, it could have been for me. This is the second bodyguard hurt because of me. What if you're next?"

Andrew rubbed Jordan's hands between his. "Tonie will be fine. My sister got a double dose of ketamine awhile back. Getting them to the hospital quick is what matters." Andrew coaxed her out of the car.

"But what if she's not fine?"

Andrew didn't answer the question as he walked her inside to the couch. His phone vibrated in his pocket. *Please, be good news.* A message from dispatch with the contact information for the vet. Not bad news.

Jordan plopped down and pulled a throw pillow to her chest. "Grandma would tell me I'm being a ninny. Logically, I know I didn't cause these things to happen, yet I feel responsible. Do you ever feel that way?"

Andrew sat down next to her. "I do. Tonie is here at my request. I'm her team leader. She is well trained, and if Ben is right, then the water bottle didn't appear tampered with and there was nothing off when she entered the suite. If there was, she would have contacted us. I can't jump to any conclusions."

They sat in silence for several minutes. Andrew couldn't think of anything to distract her with.

Jordan stood. "Let's see if there's something in the kitchen. We missed dinner, and tonight is going to be a long night."

Andrew followed her into the kitchen and opened a cupboard. "I found the baby food."

"There are pot pies in the freezer. Shall I put them in the oven?"

"Not the microwave?"

Jordan turned the package over. "These are the kind in foil. No microwave directions."

"I found Mom's Oreo stash. Too bad we don't have any milk."

"There's almond milk in the cupboard next to the fridge."

Andrew grimaced. "Almond milk? This is Wisconsin. It's probably a controlled substance."

"I'm assuming ordering delivery is out. If you want milk, your choices are almond or one of the cans of formula."

"I think I'll have my Oreos with water, thank you."

Jordan set the pies on the center of a cookie sheet. "These take sixty minutes to bake. What varieties are in your mom's stash? We can play checkers with Oreos."

"Regular, double-stuff, and lemon."

"Then let's play." Jordan took the dry-erase pen from the whiteboard on the side of the fridge and drew an 8 x 8 grid on the table. She drew a squiggle every other square.

Andrew opened the bags. "Great idea."

"Plagiarized from Hearthfire Kids. We did it in a snowy-day episode when I was nine. I had to lose that game. Chocolate or lemon?"

"Chocolate."

Jordan grinned and set twelve lemon cookies in the nonsquiggled squares. Andrew did the same with his chocolate and snuck a look at his phone. No alerts.

"Set it on the table. We will both want to know if there are new messages." Jordan started the game.

Andrew followed. Jordan waited patiently, then jumped two of his cookies. She removed them from the board and ate one.

"Hey, that was my cookie."

"*Was* is the operative word. The only way to keep the chocolate cookies is to win."

Andrew was determined not to give up another cookie. Unfortunately, he lost the first game.

They were setting up the second when his phone rang.

"Hello, Ben."

"The police detective would like to speak with you and Miss Lee tonight as soon as you have time. He says wherever you are or the station will do."

Jordan froze, holding an Oreo over the board, listening. Andrew changed to speakerphone. "I'd rather not have them here. We can meet at the station."

Ben relayed the message to someone on his end. "Tonie is responding to treatment. They have her on IV fluids and are flushing out her system. Apparently it was a cocktail of things."

Andrew closed his eyes and sent a silent prayer of gratitude heavenward that the drugs hadn't been fatal. "Do they have a timeline for her release?"

"Probably in the morning. The detective can't have a coherent conversation with her yet. He mentioned Princess is receiving similar treatment."

Jordan set the cookie on the table and closed her eyes, her relief as palpable as the earlier stress.

"Thanks, Ben." Andrew ended the call. "I guess we should turn off the pies before we head to the station."

Jordan turned the stove off. "They still have twenty-seven minutes left."

"I promise we will eat before the night is over." It was a promise he hoped he could keep.

"THE ONE THING MOVIES AND television can't capture is the smell of police stations." A veteran actor had imparted that wisdom years ago, the first time Jordan appeared in a crime show. This was the only real station Jordan had ever been in, but she agreed. Stale smells of all types accented with the scent of pine cleaner assaulted her as they followed the detective back to his office. With all the clutter on the desk, she assumed it couldn't be an interrogation room.

"Thank you for coming to the station. Mr. Hastings, if you'll wait outside my office, I'd like to question Miss Lee. We don't want to contaminate witness stories."

Andrew locked gazes with Jordan for a moment before exiting. The detective closed the door. "Tell me, in your own words, what happened."

"We dropped Tonie and Princess off, then ran out to pick up some dinner."

"Do you know what time that was?"

"I didn't look at the clock. Oh, but I did do an internet search—" Jordan checked her phone, "—at 4:52 while we waited for our burgers. When we got back to the hotel, we rode the elevator. There was no one in the hall, but Hearthfire is short on guards tonight, so that wasn't unusual. Everyone wanted to go to the game. I had a bag of food, as did Andrew. I used my phone to open the door."

"Your phone?"

"Yes, the hotel has the app, so you don't need a keycard. Ben went first and started the room sweep. Anyway, Princess didn't meet me at the door, and I had food, so that was doubly unusual. I thought Tonie must have taken her on a walk. I should have waited for Ben to finish, but the bag was ripping, so I took it to the kitchen. That's when I saw them. I screamed, and Mr. Andrew had me out of the kitchen so fast I didn't even have time to think."

"Is that Mr. Andrew's job?"

"Technically he's Princess's bodyguard, but he's really there for me. Tonight, Stu asked Mr. Andrew if he would cover for the Hearthfire guards as most of them wanted to be at the game and one was sick."

"Did you notice anything odd in your apartment this morning?"

"No. We ate breakfast and went to the set around seven thirty."

"Do you know where the bottles of water came from?"

"The hotel, I assume. I haven't purchased any."

"Do you drink bottled water?"

"Rarely. I carry my own refillable water bottle. Part of my keep-the-world-green campaign."

"What about the dog groomer—or is she a bodyguard?"

How much had the detective guessed about her supposed groomer? "Tonie will grab a water bottle before a walk or workout."

"And her job?"

"Officially she's employed by Hastings Security as my dog groomer."

The detective shut his notebook. "Thanks for coming in. I will let you know when we learn anything."

"Have you found out who put the photo with the knife on my balcony?"

"Sorry, no. And before you read about it in the papers, you

should know the shooter from the airport died this afternoon without ever giving us a statement."

Jordan put her hand over her racing heart. "Died, how?"

"Terminal cancer. To be honest, his doctor was surprised he even left the house."

"Are you sure he's the shooter, then?"

The detective shook his head. "We're reviewing everything. In the meantime, I suggest you get more security and don't stay at the hotel."

"That was my plan."

Jordan traded places with Andrew and waited for what seemed longer than she should have. They left the station in silence.

"Do you want to finish reheating the pot pies or pick something else up?" asked Andrew.

"Can we get some ice cream to go with the pies?"

Andrew frowned. "I'd rather not go into a store."

"Ponytail and hat?"

Andrew pulled into a chain-store lot. "Let's hurry."

"I know the drill. Keep my head down and don't make eye contact." Jordan pulled her hair back and put on a Cubs cap from the stash in the back seat.

Andrew scanned the lot before getting out of the car.

They made it to the checkout without incident. Andrew blocked the view of the tabloids with her photo on the cover until she passed. She added a candy bar to the ice cream. She'd worry about the extra calories later, though she knew stress eating could end a career.

As Andrew handed the cashier a twenty, the little girl in line behind them yelled and pointed. "Look, Dad, she's a princess!"

Heads turned.

Andrew threw an arm around Jordan's waist and pulled her close. Instinctively, Jordan turned into his shoulder. Andrew brushed a kiss across her brow. "I knew I had the best girlfriend, but, wow, a princess!"

The adults smiled and turned back to minding their own business. The cashier handed Andrew his change and kept studying Jordan. The little girl's father frowned. Jordan wished she could tell the child she had a good eye, but that could quickly get out of hand.

Andrew handed her the grocery sack. "Do you mind carrying this?"

With one arm wrapped around her, he must want the other one free. Jordan took the bag without looking back at the little girl.

Safely in the car, Jordan pulled out her candy bar. "I wish I was one of those people who carried their own publicity photos around. I'd wait for that girl and give her one. No one at school will believe her."

Andrew pulled a Sharpie out of the center console. "Sign the candy bar. They're coming out of the store. You can hand it to her through the window."

Jordan signed her name as Andrew pulled up behind the car where the father and daughter had stopped, and rolled down his window, "Excuse me, sir?"

The father stepped closer. His daughter held his hand. Jordan took off her hat. "Sweetheart, you have a very good eye. I'm not a princess, but sometimes I play one on TV."

"I knew you were Princess Sam!"

"Yes. I was trying to sneak in and out of the store with no one recognizing me. You won." Jordan handed the candy bar to Andrew, who handed it to the father.

The father read the signature, then narrowed his eyes. "Well, thank you. I appreciate you letting her know she wasn't making things up. But I still want her to understand it isn't polite to behave like that."

Andrew let the car roll forward a few inches, and the man backed off.

Jordan waved, and Andrew rolled up the window.

"Thanks for letting me do that. I felt so bad when I realized she was holding back the tears."

Andrew nodded. "I understand. It's hard the first time you meet a princess."

"Have you met many?"

"Just two." A half smile teased Andrew's face as if there were a hidden joke somewhere behind it.

Andrew took several unnecessary roads getting back to September's rental. After today, he would insist on a full security detail up here. Let the lawyers deal with the contract. The worst thing was that he couldn't be a part of that crew. His phone rang as he turned onto the safe house's street. He tapped the phone icon on the console.

"Mr. Andrew, this is dispatch. The team we routed back to you is having car problems and is waiting for a tow. Deidre plans to leave within the hour with Adam. They will pick up the rest of the team. Their ETA is close to 1:00 a.m."

"Thank you. Anything more?"

"Ben called. Tonie should be released in the morning. Also, the vet says Princess should sleep off the effects of the drugs and they will monitor her overnight. As a side note, one of the K-9s has made himself her personal protector. The vet says she's in good hands—and paws."

Someone was finding humor in things. Andrew checked Jordan's reaction. A sad smile was better than no smile, right? "Thanks. Tell everyone to drive safely."

"Will do."

Andrew pulled into the garage. "Shall we see if we can get as far as eating dinner?"

"I keep hoping someone will yell 'Cut!' so I can go home and get to bed." Jordan didn't wait for him to get to her door.

The Hastings app showed no security alerts for the house, but Andrew did a quick walk-through anyway. By the time he came back, Jordan had restarted the pot pies. "We forgot milk."

"Does that mean no more checkers?"

Jordan sat at the table. "I'll be chocolate this time."

Andrew noted Jordan's changed demeanor. It was close to her real self, only controlled. "Is this what you really want to do?"

"Of course."

Lifting a lemon cookie, Andrew studied Jordan's face rather than the makeshift checkerboard. "You don't need to act around me. Tonight has been traumatic. It's okay to be the real Jordan."

Jordan shrugged and moved a strand of hair over her shoulder. "You are the first person to call me on that in a long time. I think it used to be more obvious when I was little."

Andrew set his cookie down.

"I started playing different roles when my parents disappeared. The media as a whole was super invasive. Pretending I was someone else came naturally, and I could always pretend that Mom and Dad would be home at any moment. I used to watch *Gilligan's Island* reruns and imagine them trying to get off some deserted isle. Now when I need courage, I slip into different roles. I do it more than I thought. But even when I'm acting, I'm still me. I'm just me playing a role." Jordan moved a cookie.

It was too early in the game to have much strategy. Andrew took his time with his move so he could process what she was saying. "At first I thought it was weird that you played roles when you were stressed. Then I realized everyone does it. The last people you want to play poker with are a bunch of bodyguards. We can wear a blank face like no one else."

They played in silence for several rounds. "Blake uses a blank face, but there's a twitch around his left eye when he's hiding something." Jordan hopped one of his checkers and held it up to her mouth. "My dietitian is going to be on me like a drill instructor when I get home."

"No comment." Andrew moved one of his last pieces.

"And there's your bodyguard face." Hop, hop, hop. "I won." She covered her mouth as she yawned.

Andrew gathered up the remaining cookies and wiped the board off the table. "After we eat, you can use September's room. I'll be down here until the rest of the team shows up."

Jordan pulled the pot pies out of the oven. "Dinner, such as it is."

"Not used to this fare?"

"I have a nutritionist in LA who plans most of my meals." Jordan cut her pie in half. "I'm already way over her recommended daily calorie intake with the cookie games."

Andrew transferred his pie to a plate.

After they finished their meal, Jordan yawned again. "Do you think September has an extra toothbrush?"

"I have one. Just a moment." Out in the garage, Andrew pulled his go-bag out of his trunk, glad he'd restocked it.

Jordan waited in the living room. "What is that?"

"My go-bag. I keep one in my trunk at all times." He set it on the coffee table and pulled out a bag of travel-sized toiletries. "Take anything you need. I have an open toothbrush in another bag. You might need these. I'm sure the shorts are too big, but they have a drawstring." He set the pile next to his bag, mostly so he didn't have to touch her. Jordan brought out a distinctly unprofessional side of him.

She held up the dark-blue Hastings security T-shirt. It reached halfway to her knees. Andrew pushed the image from his mind. The last thing he needed to think of was Jordan in bed in his shirt.

"Thank you. I wasn't looking forward to sleeping in my clothes since I have to wear them again tomorrow."

"I can text Deidre and have her pick up something at an all-night big-box store."

"That's okay. Hopefully the detective will let me get my clothes out of the room tomorrow." Jordan held the bundle of clothes to her chest and studied him for a long moment. "Good night, Andrew, and thanks for taking care of me today."

"Good night, Jordan. Sleep well." Even if he could go to bed, he wouldn't sleep. Thoughts of Jordan would keep him awake.

IT COULD HAVE BEEN HER.

Images of Tonie and Princess lying on the hotel's green faux-tile linoleum floor wouldn't leave Jordan's mind. She rolled over again and checked the clock. Two hours of tossing and turning. Enough.

It could have been her.

Well, probably not. She rarely drank from disposable water bottles. Jordan sat up. Could it be? Was someone after her bodyguards and not her?

She tossed the covers back and ran downstairs. Andrew sat on the couch, reading a book. "I don't think someone is after me. I think they are after you."

Andrew's brows raised. "What?"

Jordan tried to clarify. The faster she talked, the more she used her hands to emphasize each word. "Not you as in Andrew, you as in my bodyguards. It's pretty well-known that I don't use disposable water bottles. It's on my website, Instagram, everything. Tonie often carries a disposable with her. So the water bottle was meant for her, not me. Then the shooting. I only saw the clips the police showed me, but I think he was shooting at Blake, not me. Why else would he keep shooting after I was protected? I know it sounds crazy."

Leaning toward her, Andrew captured her waving hands, but it wasn't his grip that stopped their movement—it was the electric shock radiating up her arms.

"It doesn't sound crazy at all. I've wondered the same thing." He released her hands.

"You have? Why didn't you tell me?"

"Mostly because I don't have any evidence. Why do you think someone's after your bodyguards?"

"First, there's the change in my contract about using Hearthfire bodyguards, who, except for Stu, seem to be better at acting than guarding. Second, at the airport, only Blake was hit. In the video I saw, Blake was hit the first time before he got me to the ground. Third, I rarely use disposable water bottles. I will when the water is unsafe or tastes really bad, but I think I've only used one or two on set since getting here. Tonie sometimes refills her water bottle, but she's just as likely to use a bottled water if it's handy. If she dropped the water bottle and it spilled, then Princess would have gotten some just by licking it off the floor."

Andrew nodded. "I've been thinking the same thing. However, if your bodyguards are the target, then you are too. Because they are trying to eliminate those most likely to protect you."

"I don't want someone to hurt you."

"We talked about this before. My job is to protect you. Sometimes there isn't a choice."

"I could fire you."

Andrew hung his head and rubbed the back of his neck.

Jordan wanted to shout her frustration. Andrew didn't get it. He wasn't just a bodyguard. He was her friend—maybe more than, if they were honest. He had to have felt the same things she did. Never had a bodyguard, or even a costar, looked like he had at her earlier this evening.

He took her hand before speaking. "Is firing me going to protect you?"

"No, but it might protect you."

Andrew winced. "A couple years ago, Adam made a mistake. He started to have feelings for his principal, and one night he acted on them and kissed her. The next day he quit."

"September?"

"Adam has a lot of regrets. He says he should have talked things out more. Or rotated off the job earlier and had someone else lead the detail and not crossed the line. I think I may need to get myself rotated out of your detail."

"Because you think I have feelings for you, or because you have feelings for me?"

He bowed his head a moment before he raised his eyes to hers. "Yes?"

Jordan's heart rate jumped. "So what do we do?"

Andrew pulled lightly on the hand he held and leaned forward until their lips touched. His kiss would have easily passed the censors for a G-rating, but as Jordan leaned into him, it surpassed any kiss she'd ever filmed as her heart sped up and a feeling of joy filled her. Andrew's other hand came up and cupped the side of her face. He deepened the kiss before pulling back. All the sensations she'd only acted out were happening in real life.

Andrew rested his forehead against hers. His blue eyes burned into her soul. September needed to write that song about the Hastings's blue eyes even if they only sang it in private.

"As soon as Adam gets here, I think I need to tell him—"

"Tell him what?" the voice from the doorway caused Jordan to pull back.

Andrew continued to hold her head. "That after my first kiss with Jordan, I think I should be rotated off her detail so I don't repeat your mistakes."

Adam crossed his arms. "Considering we entered the house and you didn't notice, I'd say that's a pretty good idea."

They saw? Her first unscripted kiss in forever and she'd still had an audience? A woman and two other men appeared behind Adam. Hopefully only his brother had witnessed the embrace.

"Deidre, will you get the others set up? I need to have a private conversation with my brother and his client. I'm assuming Miss Lee is using the master suite. Assign rooms accordingly. If there is a doghouse out back, leave it for Mr. Andrew."

Adam pointed to an office with multipaned French doors. "Shall we?"

Even under his brother's glare, Andrew held her hand as they got up from the couch. The home office contained one chair behind a desk, and a small sofa.

Adam pulled out the chair. "How long?"

"How long what?" Andrew asked.

"You know." Adam sat down in the rolling chair.

"You mean how long was my first kiss with Jordan? That is a pretty invasive question."

"Tonight—is this the first time you've been distracted?"

"Tonight is the first time we've shared a kiss and I became unaware of my surroundings. I was going to talk with you about being reassigned as soon as you got here."

Adam raised a brow. "So, before when you've kissed, you've been aware of your surroundings?"

"I already told you about the one in the trailer."

"You did?" Jordan put her hand over her mouth.

Andrew turned to her. "Considering the circumstances and how angry I was over what Storm did, I felt it best to put it in the daily report that goes to Mr. Blake and our files. If there is any cause to question my actions that day, the report is written and filed."

"But it was so ..." Jordan searched for a word. *Degrading, wrong, shameful.*

"Traumatic. Which is why I filed it. Mr. Blake needed to know."

Adam's chair squeaked, and he cleared his throat. "I owe both of you an apology. I shouldn't have goaded my brother just now. Miss Lee, in case you are wondering, I didn't see the kiss, and I apologize for my rudeness. I do agree with Andrew, though. He should be off your protective detail. I can tell you from experience, it is difficult to do a proper job when you are in love with your principal."

Love? Jordan giggled to hide her nervousness at the thought. Both men looked at her. She scrambled to cover her reaction. "You know how wrong that sounds when you say principal? I think of the woman who played the principal at the elementary school in the kids show..."

Adam grinned back. "Yuck, that sounds bad. Look, guys, it's late. I'll give you a few moments alone. In the morning, we can call Mr. Blake and let him know we're changing out the detail and why. Andrew, I assume the police will want you to stay around for a couple days. We'll need to sort things out with Hearthfire. If you'll excuse me, I'll go see where Deidre has put me. Good night. Don't stay up too late." Adam shut the door as he left.

Did that mean Adam approved? He'd left them alone in a room. Granted, there were no curtains on the French doors.

Andrew stared at the door with a puzzled expression. "Do you think you'll be able to sleep now?"

Jordan felt heat flood her face. "Maybe not, but I don't think I'll be seeing Tonie on the floor anymore."

"Do you think I can get a good-night kiss?"

No one sat in the room beyond the doors. "I'd like that very much."

Andrew's and Adam's phones simultaneously rang with alarm and call sounds. Andrew's caller ID showed Mr. Blake. What had him calling at four thirty in the morning, California time? "Hello?"

"Is that what you call protecting my girl? I should have you horsewhipped. What were you thinking?"

Andrew held the phone away from his ear.

Andrew turned his phone to face Adam. Storm's video of their kiss played on the screen. "Mr. Blake, that is the incident I put in my report two weeks ago, the day it happened. I also reported how Storm intended to blackmail Jordan with the video if she didn't have brunch with him this past Sunday."

"My girl doesn't sidle up to some man like a two-dollar hussy. And you never said you participated!"

Actually, Andrew's report had been fairly detailed and included the full extent of his participation, or lack thereof. "Do you know when the video was released?"

"Does it matter?"

"Yes. Most of the country is still asleep. If we act fast, we can get it down." Andrew put his phone on speaker as he dressed.

"How?"

"It was filmed without Jordan's knowledge or consent in her trailer, where she had an expectation of privacy. The social media networks aren't going to like getting legal notices about it. Get her lawyer out of bed and get him on it. With your permission, we can run some Ogilvie software that will locate the videos and send alerts to the various companies. The big social media sites will block it out of fear of reprisal."

"Get this fixed and then you are fired. I'm flying out today." The phone call ended.

Adam held up his phone. "Already working on it. I suggest you go tell Miss Lee."

Too late. Jordan stood in the middle of the hall, staring at her phone, tears falling onto the screen.

He reached out to her.

She stepped back.

"Jordan?"

"Grandma called. It is all over the news in London. She's furious. She wants me to fire you."

"Mr. Blake said the same thing. He's flying out."

Jordan looked up from her screen. "Is he well enough?"

Andrew shrugged.

Adam yelled from the living room. "Video conference in five."

Jordan slumped against the wall. "I can't do this."

Andrew took her by the shoulders. "Yes, you can. You will get through it. I've watched you deal with some hard things these past two weeks. We can get through this."

"I mean us. I can't do us. Last night was…was…all there will ever be."

Andrew couldn't find his next breath. It was like the time his sister first had taken him down with her signature move, only he wasn't blinking at the ceiling and seeing stars this time. "We better get on that call."

Andrew followed Jordan to the living room, where she was perched on the arm of the couch next to Deidre. Andrew sat on the chair at the other side of the room. Adam's laptop was connected to the large-screen TV. The Hastings logo was replaced by a split screen. Dad sat in his home office with Mom next to him. Alan sat in his office at Hastings, switching back and forth between a half dozen monitors.

Jethro started the meeting. "I'd say good morning, but I assume it's too late for that, so let's fix this. Your mom filled me in on what she knows, and I read the incident reports. Nothing we say will change the past. Alan, where are we?"

"The Ogilvie bot traced the point of origin as, not surprisingly, an all-night restaurant in Green Bay at 3:00 am. Two of the major social media networks have removed the video. The others have yet to respond. The video was sent directly to several tabloid outlets in Great Britain as well as the United States. I sent an alert to Abbie. What her husband and Harmon media decide to do with the news is their decision. This does raise a troubling question. Timing. The poisoning or attempted murder of Tonie was set to be at the top of several of the Hollywood gossip shows and blogs today. Not surprising, and the blogs only had basic information and not Tonie's name, although they knew Princess was also under veterinary care. That wasn't exactly a story we wanted to run, but who would have wanted it to run less than Jordan?"

Jordan leaned forward. "So did Storm release it? I can't see him doing that where he can't use it as leverage."

Alan only half looked at his camera as he spoke. "According to his social media posts, Storm wasn't in the restaurant last night. He may have directed its release, or someone who had access may have released it. If his goal was to get you to go out with him, it doesn't make sense."

"The person who did this wants me fired." Andrew scooted forward in his seat. "Last night, Jordan and I started putting the incidents together. Everything has been to get rid of her body-guards. The contract, Blake's shooting ... Jordan rarely drinks from disposable water bottles, so the drugs were meant for Tonie. This gets me fired. Both Blake and Mrs. Lee are clear on that."

"Worse, it gets all of Hastings fired," said Alan.

Dad folded his arms across his chest. "I don't care if we lose this job. I don't care if Blake doesn't pay us. This is our mess to clean up, and Jordan is ours to protect. I'm not comfortable with what happens when we walk away. One bodyguard isn't enough for the ongoing threats."

"But you've been fired. Why would you keep working for me without pay?" asked Jordan.

Jethro leaned closer to the camera. "Because Andrew pulled himself off your detail this morning. If he is claiming you as his girlfriend, we are too."

"But we aren't. I told him it won't work." The strong-woman persona was back. Jordan didn't even blink.

"Nevertheless, we will sort this out," said Jethro.

"How can you help if you've been fired?" Jordan looked to each person in the room.

Deidre turned to Jordan. "Before last night, did you know who I was?"

"Only from Andrew's description."

"Who is Mr. Blake hiring to be your next bodyguard?" asked Deidre.

"I don't know. He is flying out himself. But I don't think he is ready, especially if someone is trying to take out my bodyguards. He might be bringing someone we've hired before. Where are you going with this?"

Deidre faced the laptop camera. "Mr. Blake will need backup. Dermot Security should do a bid as they are number two in Chicago. Then I work contract for them again. Jordan needs a female who can be with her 24/7. I have it on good authority that Dermot is still lacking in that area."

"But Tonie got hurt. Aren't you putting yourself in danger?" asked Jordan.

Deidre put an arm around Jordan's shoulders. "Ask the boys. I need a little action now and again."

Alan tapped away at his computer. "The video got pulled from a major viewing site. And several small sites are pulling it. Some of the British gossip sites are also pulling it."

"How do you know Storm wasn't the one to post it?" Andrew didn't believe the actor wasn't behind it.

"He was at a victory party after last night's game. There are enough time-stamped shots to give him a tight alibi." Alan turned from another screen. "You won't like this. One of the major networks is running with the story. Miss Lee, I hope you have good lawyers."

Jordan's phone rang. The color drained from her face. She stood and left the room before answering it.

Adam pointed to Deidre to follow.

She nodded and indicated she could see Jordan from where she sat.

Mom tilted the home camera in her direction. "Ben is still with Tonie, right?"

"Yes, and the dog is still at the vet," said Andrew.

"If it's safe for their health, let's get them out of there before the paparazzi descend. Did we finish the work we were contracted to do on Claire Lee's condo?"

"Yes," said one of the guards who came with Adam last night.

"Move Jordan there. Yes, I know Hearthfire knows the location." Mom waved her hand dismissively. "That lets us keep September's rental a secret. Deidre, have you already contacted Dermot about a bid?"

Deidre looked up from her phone. "Just texted Liam. They're working on something to approach Mr. Blake with now."

Jethro turned the camera back to face him. "Good. Andrew, stay in town as long as you can. The one thing everyone will believe at the moment is that you are the boyfriend, even if Jordan says otherwise. It's on days like this I wished one of us had become a private investigator."

Andrew gave a two-finger salute to his father. Staying with Jordan would be torturous given her announcement, but he'd do whatever it took to keep her safe.

A pale-faced Jordan walked zombie-like back into the room. Andrew ran around the couch, but Deidre beat him to Jordan. "What's wrong?" they asked in unison.

Alan answered from the computer screen. "A fishing vessel out of Kiribati claims to have found the remains of a small passenger plane. Tentatively, it has been identified as the plane carrying Jordan's parents."

Jordan launched herself into Andrew's arms. "It has to be a cruel joke."

With one hand on her back, Andrew moved Jordan to the hallway and away from the prying eyes of his family.

Kiribati? THE NAME SOUNDED FAMILIAR. Jordan pulled away from Andrew and opened her phone. According to the map app, the island nation sat too far south of the registered flight plan. No way could it be the right plane. It wasn't the first time a hoax finding had occurred, and it wouldn't be the last. Someone must have realized that she was at the top of the news cycle and wanted to cash in on their five minutes of fame. The chance that it was the plane that carried her father and mother on a medical mission trip to the Philippines was minimal.

Jordan's phone played the theme song to one of Claire Lee's most famous movies. Jordan rushed upstairs, needing privacy before she answered. "Hello, Grandma."

"We are not having a very good day, are we?"

Jordan sat on the end of the bed. "No. Do you think it's Mom and Dad?"

"I doubt it. But I do hope someone will find peace in having their loved ones found. Every story needs an end."

If only their story had an end.

Grandma continued. "I should be there late afternoon tomorrow. Blake says you're moving to my condo."

The move had been decided on only moments ago. Hastings Security was on top of things. "The local police have requested I don't stay in the hotel. Paul must comply." That conversation would not be fun.

"Not sure about that. Your contract for this last season is rather convoluted. I'll get Donetta and our lawyer on it. Now, about that boy…"

"Andrew Hastings or that snake, Storm Tordon?"

"The bodyguard. Mrs. Blake says he did his duty and reported the incident when it happened. She says his report reads almost as long as the video clip. It's much longer than the explanation you gave me. Have you fired him yet?"

"Blake fired him."

"I'm not sure that was the right move."

"It doesn't matter. Andrew is leaving my detail today anyway and turning it over to his brother." He was leaving for her, but she'd pushed him away.

"Why would he quit?"

Jordan weighed her options. Lying would be easier, but Grandma would be here in two days or less and see the truth. "Because we don't have a traditional bodyguard/client relationship."

There was a long pause. "I warned you about this. What did you do?"

"A lot of late-night phone calls, and then we could laugh together, and last night we kissed. I know you warned me. It just happened. But I told him this morning there can be no us."

"Well, at least he had the decency to leave you."

"He says he can't guard me well if his emotions are engaged."

The pause was longer this time. "I don't know what to say. You've heard my lectures, yet one thing you said gives me pause."

"What was that?"

"You said you laugh together. With everything going on, if he is bringing laughter into your life, I'm not sure what to think."

Jordan let out a breath she didn't realize she had been holding. "I assume last night's kiss wasn't anything like the video."

"No. Definitely not. It was sweet." And he kissed me. Jordan wanted to turn that thought over and over. Their first real kiss.

However, Grandma kept talking. "I want to meet him. Don't let him leave before I get there."

Great. Another disaster in the making. "His family is amazing. Even though Blake fired Hastings, they have been rallying around me, working out a security plan, and making sure I have the best bodyguards available. They are trying to get their number-one competitor to bid for the job with Blake. Who does that?"

"Their competitor? You're sure?"

"I'm not sure of the dynamics. They seem to have a working relationship of sorts."

"Should I encourage Blake to take the bid?"

"Either that or stay with Hastings. Andrew did nothing wrong the day of the video. It was my choice to take Storm's stupid dare. Andrew didn't even kiss me back."

"Do you like this bodyguard?"

It was Jordan's turn for a long pause. "I dumped him. It doesn't matter."

"I'll give Blake a call. Bye, bunny."

"Love you."

Jordan lay back on her bed and stared at the ceiling. Her phone rang again. Reggie. Jordan ignored the request for a video and chose audio-only.

"Where are you?"

"I'm in a safe house."

"The police have been asking questions all morning. Did someone really kill your bodyguard? He was so hot."

"If the police are questioning you, I don't think I should answer. But I can say that no one is dead."

"Oh, good. That would have been a shame if he'd died. Then what about your parents' plane?"

"Reggie, I know you want all the tea, but I'm not up to speaking about the last few hours. How was the game?"

"Cold. I think we all had a few too many drinks at the after-party. I have such a headache this morning. Kittie was so funny last night. I think Storm might have taken her back to his place. She wasn't here this morning."

"I didn't think Storm liked her."

"Me neither. Oh, someone is knocking on my door. I better go."

The call ended. Jordan went to the bathroom and fixed her face. Ready or not, she needed to go out and face the Hastings group and Andrew. Out of habit, her mind reached for a character her grandmother had played in a movie in 1972. The role was one Jordan often used when she needed to be stronger than she was. She stopped herself. Andrew would see through it. Maybe she should just go downstairs as herself. She was strong enough.

Andrew sat across from Jordan in the living room of Claire Lee's condo. Even though he was no longer on duty, he found he was aware of everything, from Adam and Deidre talking quietly in the kitchen to the third car to park in the lot in a half hour. The police had released the hotel room, and Adam sent two body-guards to pack it up. Ben and Tonie met them there to do the job.

Tonie had suffered only a mild headache and an uncalled-for case of embarrassment. She'd also sworn off bottled water for the rest of her existence.

Princess lay curled up at Jordan's feet. According to the vet, the dog might be extra sleepy for the next day or two. Andrew refrained from asking how they could tell if a dog who spent twenty hours a day sleeping was extra sleepy. So far, the media hadn't found Jordan, although several interview requests had come through her agent.

Jordan set her phone down. "Blake's plane landed."

Adam and Deidre came from the kitchen. Deidre had changed into a dark-blue suit.

"Dermott Security met Blake at the airport. He says he wants to talk with Hastings before signing a contract," said Deidre. "Simon Dermot agreed to add me to lead his team if they are hired. Liam is up here to negotiate only. I don't work on Liam's details. I'll stay in the background. That way, whoever Blake chooses to work with, I'll be their employee. I hope Blake will jump at the chance to have a female on guard duty."

"I know Blake isn't going to give me much choice, but I like your plan. Andrew told me a lot about your background. You probably cringe in every show where I use martial arts," said Jordan.

"I cringe at most shows where actors attempt to use martial arts. I haven't seen any of yours specifically."

"You're lucky. I only trained through green belt, so I mostly mimic the choreographers' moves."

"Maybe I can teach you a few things." A wicked smile flashed across Deidre's face.

Adam looked just as horrified as Andrew felt.

Jordan studied all three of them. "I think I missed an inside joke."

"As much as not one Hastings brother wants to admit. In hand-to-hand combat, Deidre can win most any day." Adam hung his head.

"I'm going outside so I can come in after Blake gets here so it isn't obvious whose team I'm on." Deidre left through the back door.

Jordan rested her hands in her lap. "I feel underhanded using Deidre this way. But to have made some deal with your competitor, she must be good."

"Dermot security would love to steal her away." Adam sat down in the chair nearest the door.

"They won't have to try too hard once she marries Liam." Andrew turned to face Jordan. "Liam and Deidre fell in love on a joint assignment to keep Abbie and her triplets safe during the delivery. I'm not 100 percent sure if they are officially engaged or not, but for now, Deidre still works for us."

"So they guard your sister. That explains how you could work with another firm," said Jordan.

"Dermot Security's biggest client happens to be the Harmons. Since they guard Abbie, we are motivated to keep good relations." Adam checked his phone and went to the door. He opened it before Blake knocked.

Blake looked first to Jordan. Issuing a wordless challenge, he frowned as his eyes locked on Andrew's. "I thought you'd be gone." Even with his arm in a sling, Blake looked intimidating.

"I'm not here as part of Jordan's detail." Andrew cleared his throat. "Claire Lee asked that I stay to meet her."

"What?"

Jordan grabbed Andrew's hand. "Blake, I assumed you talked with Grandma."

Blake continued to glare. "I'd hoped she was wrong about this. Don't get mixed up with your bodyguards. I've told you that before."

"No, you told me not to get mixed up with men who don't have my welfare in mind. Andrew has put me first every single time."

"What about that video?"

Andrew looked Blake in the eye. "Did you read my report?"

"Yes."

"Then you know why I made the choices I made. It's unfortunate the video is out there. We have a theory I hope you'll consider before you decide who to hire to help with Jordan's security while she finishes filming." Andrew explained how they thought someone was after Jordan's bodyguards and that the video was released to get Andrew fired from Jordan's detail.

Blake sat down in a straight-backed chair. "I see your point. If I don't fire Hastings, does that mean they will go to greater lengths to get rid of you?"

Andrew didn't like the thought of greater lengths. "I don't know. Whoever it is either knew Tonie wasn't a dog groomer or wanted her out of Jordan's suite."

"Or they wanted Jordan out of the hotel. The black roses and the photograph on the balcony would have made me move Jordan under normal circumstances." Blake frowned. "Claire will be here tomorrow. She's been traveling with a team of four. Since I normally contract out the rest of our teams, I need to hire someone. The lawyers are trying to see what can be done with the contract. Apparently, the private-security-personnel issue has to do with Storm's contract."

"What?" most everyone in the room asked.

Blake shrugged. "I'm not a lawyer. Just repeating what they said. The staying-in-the-same-hotel thing was Paul's idea. Hearthfire is releasing Jordan from staying with the rest of the cast and crew since the police have asked her not to stay there."

"My contract only refers to bodyguards on the sets, not my personal life, right?" asked Jordan.

Mr. Blake nodded. "I think so."

"Since I'm not with the rest of the cast and crew, the only issue is on set security. Princess isn't allowed up at the mansion. And even in LA, I can't have a bodyguard in the studio. So I need a detail for offset, as well as a driver. Most likely the driver can stay around at the mansion or studio."

"True." Blake looked around the room and pointed at Deidre. "Who do you work for?"

"That depends. I have a rather fluid working relationship with both Hastings and Dermott."

Blake scowled at her answer and turned to Andrew. "To be clear, I still want to knock your block off, but Claire told me not to hurt you. Regardless of who I hire, are you staying around?"

"I'm not sure." As much as Andrew wanted to be near Jordan, his staying would be difficult for both of them.

Blake got up and circled the room, stopping in front of every guard and looking them in the eye. He paused in front of Deidre. "I'm hiring you. Since you are some sort of free agent, I assume you can pull a team together."

"The best one in Chicago."

"Do it." Blake turned to Andrew. "Which condo is the operations base?"

"The north one. We also rented the south one for extra room."

"Good. You can show me the way, and we can have a chat." He held out his arm to Jordan. "I'll take that hug now and any silly blather you have to say in this boy's defense."

Jordan gave Blake a hug and whispered in his ear. Blake shook his head when he stepped back. "Come on, Andrew, show me to the condo."

Jordan stared at the closed door. The choice to end things with Andrew bothered her. Perhaps it was because he was still here. Normally, couples didn't stay near each other after a breakup.

Adam sat down in the spot Andrew had vacated. "That talk will go better than you assume."

Deidre paced the room. "So, I guess I get to try out my dream of running my own firm. I'd like access to Hastings software since it's already attached to the security in this house. Andrew is Hastings' best driver, but he can't be on the team."

Jordan excused herself, confident her input was no longer needed. Princess followed her into the kitchen. The refrigerator hadn't been stocked yet, and the cupboards were bare. As Jordan sat at the table to write out a list of the foods she wanted, the door to the single-car garage opened and Tonie came in, followed by Ben, who was carrying the suitcases.

"How do you feel?" asked Jordan.

Tonie sat down in the chair opposite Jordan. Princess circled her chair. "Stupid. I can't believe I didn't even look for signs of tampering. Had I not guzzled almost the entire bottle, I might have realized something was wrong faster. Sorry about Princess. I gave her a bit of my water in her bowl before I started drinking."

"I'm glad the damage wasn't worse."

"I had Ben record me packing your things." Tonie handed Jordan her phone.

Jordan pushed the phone away. "You didn't need to do that. I trust you."

"That isn't why. I know the police went through the room, but if anything is missing, it might be easier to figure it out from where it was in the room."

"Oh." Jordan took the phone and watched the video, pausing it to rewind through her underwear drawer. Everything was there, plus a sense of violation. Underwear drawers did not belong in videos. Plus, knowing the police had searched through her room didn't help. Something was wrong in the next drawer. Jordan replayed it. "Did you see a baby-blue scarf with pink flowers?"

"The one you wore last Tuesday?"

"Yes, that one."

"Could you have left it at the trailer?"

"Maybe." Jordan watched the rest of the video. "The scarf is the only thing missing besides the toothbrush you questioned when you went through my things. I know this is crazy, but if someone poisoned the water, could they have done something to my makeup?"

Tonie looked at Ben. Ben nodded. "It is possible."

"The police didn't check it?"

Jordan handed the phone back. "Perhaps we should throw it away—and yours too. I'll pay for new makeup."

"Should we get it tested?" asked Tonie.

"My gut says better to know how far someone would go." Ben left the room.

Tonie followed him with her eyes. "I have a mandatory week of paid leave. It's been nice working with you. I hope nothing else happens."

"You and me both."

Tonie exited the room.

Jordan finished her shopping list, then went online to replace her makeup. Some local department store would probably carry most of the items, but she could only picture a random bodyguard having to pick it up.

Andrew came into the kitchen. "There you are."

"You survived?"

"Blake and I reached an understanding."

"Do I need to check on him?"

Andrew shook his head. "No, we're both good."

"I wish I could have witnessed this chat."

Andrew's face grew pink.

"Are you blushing?" asked Jordan.

"No."

"Now I'm curious."

"You might not like it. He agreed to let me stay until your agent and publicist decide what to do about the video. Even though it isn't viral, it's still out there. Claiming me as a boyfriend may work out better than a denial. After all, you were not scantily clad. And nothing other than the out-of-character crawl is scandalous about the clip."

"But I asked you to leave. Would you stay and pretend to be my boyfriend?"

Andrew turned one of the kitchen chairs backward and straddled it. "Am I pretending?"

"I dumped you."

"Did you, or were you scared of continuing?"

Jordan took a deep breath. She was terrified. Their relationship had no script. "I don't know where continuing goes."

"No one ever does. Life isn't a movie script."

She mulled Andrew's answer over. "I dumped you just ten hours ago. Doesn't it make me fickle to ask you back?"

Andrew folded his arms across the back of the seat and rested his chin on them. "Did you want to dump me this morning, or was it a reaction to the video?"

Jordan doodled on her grocery list. "I've missed you all day and wished I could have a do-over." She raised her eyes to meet his. "May I?"

"Have a do-over?"

She nodded.

"I'd like that." He smiled, and they sat in silence.

The sense of unbalance Jordan had carried with her all day started to fade. Andrew reached over and took her hand.

"Back to the video kiss..." He rubbed his thumb over her knuckles.

Jordan closed her eyes and thought about the kiss Storm had orchestrated. Chances were, the censors would be hard-pressed to give the kiss a PG-13 rating. "You're right." Jordan found the contact number for Donetta. "Hey, it's Jordan. I have an idea, or rather, we have an idea. I think I should just claim Andrew is my boyfriend and say he was helping me rehearse a scene. That the video was a joke."

"What good would that accomplish?"

"It kills the story, and it's true."

"What?" asked her agent.

"I'm dating my former bodyguard. The only story in the video is me acting very un-me-ish. There are probably five actresses who've posted more risqué selfies of themselves in the last hour. We take away the story, and it dies."

"Hmmm. I like it. Would he be comfortable with a few candid shots? A walk in the park or something?"

Jordan looked at Andrew before answering. "I think we can do that."

"Get me two photos ASAP in two different outfits and locations, and I can make this story die. You actually dating someone is news."

Jordan hung up the phone. "Could you hear that?"

"Enough to know we're going on a photo date. Dog park?"

"That and a selfie in the car should do it."

As she ran upstairs, Jordan realized she hadn't been trying to act like anyone else, which was good because only her real self should have Andrew for a boyfriend.

24

FOR ANDREW, THE BEST THING about Claire Lee being on set was that she wasn't always watching him. In the five days since she'd arrived last Saturday, Andrew had been subjected to a number of stare downs. The second-best thing was that her bodyguards were now allowed on the set. So, for the last three days of filming, he hadn't spent much time worrying about Jordan when she was at work. Instead, he threw himself into retracing every clue he had access to, hoping to find the source of the threat, which, sadly, was not proving very successful.

The missing blue scarf had not shown up and was added to the police report. Andrew's conversation with the detective didn't produce any new information.

Andrew checked the time. Filming should have ended for the day out at the mansion. He had only an hour before Jordan would be back and he could eat dinner with her while answering another one hundred questions about his background for her grandmother. The woman had missed her calling in life. She should have been an FBI interrogator.

As he was combing the internet for anything that might have been missed in connection with Jordan, a news story about the plane wreck found near Kiribati appeared. A special British diving team had been called in. They'd confirmed it was the right model of plane but had no new information.

Jordan and Claire Lee had released a carefully worded statement at a Sunday-afternoon press conference, the tone matching that of similar press releases over the years. They reminded the public that over fifty people, including the pilot and crew, had disappeared that day and that they should be remembering them and others hurting from various tragedies around the world. After the initial shock, Jordan hadn't mentioned the discovery of the plane.

The Lees had kept a list of the families of the missing. Those on the flight included nurses, doctors, and a crew filming a documentary, including the son of an actor Andrew had never heard of. If the Lees hadn't been on the plane, it would be largely forgotten to anyone but relatives by now. He found no link between them and the people around Jordan now.

A new set of search terms produced another video of the airport shooting and the aftermath. It was by a local blogger interviewing fans about what happened. It wasn't the interviewee that caught his attention but the girl in the background signing to her mother.

Andrew picked up the phone. "Alan, I'm sending you a video. There's a girl in a wheelchair signing to her mom. The angle isn't great, and the resolution is blurry. Can you enhance it?"

"If I can't, I'll see if Colin Ogilvie can. Alex says he was asking for test footage for some new project." The technological partner of C & O Enterprises often partnered with Hastings Security to develop new safety systems. Since Mr. Ogilive was also a Hastings client, the collaborations which resulted in better security, like the Hastings app, benefited both parities.

"Thanks. Also, if we can identify the girl, it would be helpful." Finding the signing child would be a long shot, even for Alan.

Andrew disconnected the call and watched the video again.

Someone knocked on his bedroom door.

"Come in."

The door opened, and Jordan leaned against the doorjamb. "I can't—unless you want to experience Blake's version of a shotgun wedding."

Andrew grabbed his computer. "You're back earlier than I expected."

"We're actually late. I even texted you."

"You did?" Andrew led the way to the living area, where he set the laptop down and checked his phone. He'd missed her text and another one from Alan saying the video was done. "Sorry. I think I found something, and I was concentrating so hard I must have blocked everything out. I want you to watch something."

Jordan sat down next to him, and Andrew played the video Alan had sent.

"That's Hannah."

He stopped the video. "You know her?"

"I met her right before the shooting."

"Tell me what you think she's saying to her mom."

Andrew resumed the video. It was much clearer, but some of Hannah's frantic signing was still hard to understand.

"Police…wrong man…purple shirt…" Jordan shook her head. "Sorry, I'm not that good, and it's like she's signing the same thing over and over."

Andrew texted Alan the girl's name. "I would love to talk to her. She seems to have seen something others missed. Maybe because she couldn't hear the gunshots or the screaming, she didn't duck and hide."

"The police probably didn't have an interpreter when they did their interviews, so they probably didn't question her either. I wonder if we can find her." Jordan looked at her vibrating phone. "After dinner. Grandma is wondering where we are."

"Tell her we're making out."

Jordan covered her mouth and laughed. "That would be a lie."

Andrew leaned in and stole a quick kiss. "Not necessarily."

She slapped his shoulder. "Come on, it's our last night with Grandma."

And the end of the long, soul-searching stares.

Jordan was scrolling through her phone, looking for a new book, when Grandma tapped on the door and let herself in. "Got a moment?"

"Sure." Jordan scooted over on her bed.

Grandma sat down and arranged her robe just so. "He passed."

Jordan dropped her phone. "What? Who passed? Blake?"

"No. Andrew. He passed my tests."

"You scared me. I thought you meant dying."

"I'm sorry. I thought you realized I was testing him."

"A gazillion questions, ten o'clock curfew, and some of the most difficult foods to eat? Yes, it's crossed my mind that you've been trying to torture my boyfriend."

"I'll leave the torturing to Blake. He's more protective of you than most fathers are."

"He had a *chat* with Andrew last Friday when he got here. All I know is that there was no bloodshed. Although I don't think Andrew would have thrown any punches if there were."

"I made Blake read the incident report of the kissing clip aloud to me. By the time he reached the end, he'd cooled off considerably."

"What did it say?" Jordan needed to get a copy of that report.

"At the end, Andrew put in an apology to you and us for not finding a better way to circumvent the matter, especially not knowing what an emotional toll it would exact from you."

"Bodyguards don't normally write apologies, do they? Especially when it was my choice. I could have told Storm to take a long hike off the closest pier and Andrew would have walked him down to the docks."

"Your idea about telling the truth that Andrew is a boyfriend worked."

"I know. We have been ducking paparazzi all week. He's good at it. Gives them a couple of photos and no comment as he whisks me away. I guess he's seen enough of it to not even be flustered."

"Have you given any thought to what happens when filming is over and you go back to LA?" Grandma smoothed her robe out again.

"We haven't talked about it. But then, we haven't had much unsupervised time this week." Jordan tossed a small throw pillow at Grandma, who easily caught it.

"You only have ten more days of taping. Paul is eager to wrap up ahead of schedule, even if he doesn't get the snowfall he planned on getting."

"I'm just glad I'm done with my scenes kissing Storm. Today's wedding scene went smoother because you were there. He muttered something about real grandmothers."

"He doesn't respect me for being your grandmother, only that he knows I know everyone who is everyone within a degree or two of separation, including Kevin Bacon." Grandma paused. "You kids don't play that game, do you?"

Jordan shrugged. "I've heard of it. Apparently I rate a two on the scale because you appeared in that one film with him. But I never played it."

"Remind me to invite Kevin to your wedding. Then you can add a one to that list."

"Grandma, you wouldn't! Besides, I think I have to appear in a movie with him."

"True. You still have time, then."

Jordan shivered. "That's just weird. I'm not making that one of my filmography goals."

"Worse goals have been made in Hollywood." Grandma's face grew grim. "I suppose you heard the British are diving to the wreck today."

"Yes. I'm trying to not think about it. I hope it is them. I'm tired of having the story come up every couple years."

"At least this isn't some sighting on a remote island. Those are the hardest. I accepted my son's death years ago. I detest the press questioning my decisions to have Hirst and Ellen declared dead or our annual memorial so they can find a new angle."

Jordan took her grandma's hand. "I know. I wonder if it's easier for the other families. No one calls them for interviews or waits to catch them outside of work."

"It could be harder for them. Every time we're on TV, it could seem like everyone else forgot their loss."

They sat in silence for a minute, then Grandma leaned over and kissed Jordan's cheek. "I should let you get some sleep. You have to film tomorrow. The real reason I came in was to tell you I'm staying for a couple more days. I'd rather be together when we hear the news. If you want, I can hang around the set and keep Storm in line."

"You don't need to. I think he got the message. However, may I have an extended curfew tonight?" To think she had a curfew at this age. It was more out of respect for Grandma and work demands that she and Andrew kept their late nights to a minimum.

"I can arrange that." Grandma smiled. "I really like him. Good night."

"Love you." Jordan squeezed her grandma and watched her leave. As soon as the door closed, she texted Andrew.

Grandma was testing you! And you passed.
—Did she give me a grade?
No, but she said you're a keeper.
—:) Alan found Hannah. Do you think she would meet with you?
Probably. She was pretty excited when we talked at the airport. I don't really want to set it up through my publicist. Maybe you can set it up and we can visit her after school.
—I'll call her mother tomorrow and see if I can set something up for after you're done filming.

FYI, Grandma is staying two or three more days. The Brits dove for the plane today, and we want to be together for the news. There have been over eighty vanished flights with over fifteen passengers worldwide since World War II, so the chances that this is the right plane are remote.

—**You've quoted those statistics before.**

Jordan stared at the unexpected response. **I guess I have. The good thing is that, usually, the divers are able to identify the wreckage pretty fast.**

—**Then you stop reciting the facts until the next news story.**

Pretty much.

—**That's a hard way to live.**

Jordan swallowed, glad they weren't on video chat and relieved Andrew had never placated her or pitied her.

—**Do you want me around when you hear the news?**

You realize that means you hang out with Grandma tomorrow?

—**Yes. When she isn't grilling me, she has fun stories.**

Yes, I'd like you around.

—**I'll be there.**

Good night.

—**Hugs. Sleep well.**

Jordan put her phone away and laughed because she hadn't taken advantage of a later curfew. That night, she slept the best she had since leaving LA nearly four weeks ago.

CLAIRE LEE SET HER CARDS down and answered her phone. Andrew stood to leave and give her some privacy, but the octogenarian actress waved him back as she thanked whoever had called. "It's the right plane. They're contacting the families before the press conference in four hours."

"What would you like me to do?"

"Get Jordan off the set now."

Andrew dialed Deidre's number and relayed the request. Claire went into the other room and started making a few calls of her own.

Andrew's phone played the song he'd programmed in last night as Jordan's ring.

"They found them?"

"That's what your grandmother said."

"I can't believe it."

"Are you coming back here?"

Jordan's laugh was too high-pitched to be real. "Deidre walked on set midscene. Paul is still yelling. Oh, I need to get this dress back to wardrobe."

Paul would follow them here. "One moment, Jordan." Andrew entered the living room, where Claire was finishing a call. "They have Jordan. Hastings has a safe house Hearthfire doesn't know about. Would you two like to go to that location?"

"Oh, that would give us a little privacy. Yes, please."

"Jordan, tell Deidre to take you to September's rental. We'll meet you there."

"Will you grab a change of clothing for me?"

"Anything in particular?"

"A sweater and jeans."

"Okay, see you in a few."

As Andrew opened Jordan's closet, he called Alan and asked him to put the rental on active-use status. He met Claire in the living room. "Does your driver want to follow me, or would you rather come in my car?"

Claire's bodyguard answered. "Blake and I will ride with you and Mrs. Lee. The others will stay here. Having a presence here will throw off the media."

"I'll get my car." Andrew ran across the lot, glad he'd taken the time to scrape the ice from his windows that morning. Other cars still glistened white where the frost touched them.

Andrew pulled into September's garage a half minute before Deidre. Caught between being a bodyguard and a boyfriend, he waited while Jordan and Claire hugged and walked into the house, which Deidre had cleared.

Jordan entered the kitchen, and Andrew pulled her into a hug. "What do you need?"

"Grandma and I just need the office for a while. We have calls to make. Our agent already has a statement drafted in case the plane was ever found. It will need to be updated. Did you get an appointment with Hannah?"

"Her mother said she has early release on Friday. We have an appointment tomorrow at 3:00 p.m."

"Good. I'd better go in with Grandma." Jordan gave Andrew a kiss on the cheek before leaving.

Deidre met him in the living room. "Stu called demanding to

know where Jordan is. The paparazzi are at the studio. I told him she was safe with Claire."

"So much for the story waiting." Andrew sat on the couch and pulled out his laptop. "They will probably want to make a statement. Where can we hold a press conference?"

"A hotel meeting room or ballroom. Usually, both have multiple access points. Possibly a stage area. I'm looking in Dermot's files to see if they have ever worked a venue here. I asked Alan to check Hastings."

Blake and Mrs. Lee's bodyguards appeared to be doing the same thing.

Andrew kept an eye on the office. Neither Jordan nor her grandmother seemed emotional as they made phone calls. The bodyguards shared information and narrowed the list of venues down to two possibilities.

Claire Lee came out, followed by Jordan. "The syndicated news outlets all want us in their affiliate studios. I've told them that won't work." She turned to her head of security. "Have you found a suitable location?"

"We found two locations. The first is at the Hotel Northland downtown. The second—"

Mrs. Lee held up her hand. "Just set up the one you prefer. I don't want to have to make a choice."

"Hotel Northland. Built in the 1920s and recently renovated. The ballroom is not being used until a wedding tomorrow afternoon. The planner I spoke with said they have the chairs set up, which will work for a press conference. They can either bring in a podium or have headset microphones, if you prefer."

Jordan and her grandmother shared a look, then Jordan spoke. "I have an idea for trying to make it look homey. Can they bring in two chairs, wing-back if possible, and a small table with flowers? And we'll use the headset mics."

Blake was on his phone before Jordan finished her description.

"We also need to change clothes. How can we do that without having the media on our heels?"

Deidre stood. "I can book you a suite at the hotel. Your driver is at the condo and can meet us at the hotel with what you need."

"I'll call Maria. She can meet us there for hair and makeup. Grandma might not need it, but my nerves have me shaking, and I don't want to poke my eye out with a mascara wand." Jordan's laugh was too high-pitched to not be forced.

There was mild laughter around the room.

"Let's get this done." Claire marched to the garage as the bodyguards, including Andrew, scrambled to keep up.

The one-way window allowed Jordan a view into the ballroom. The hotel's event planner had arranged two stately upholstered chairs in the front corner. An old-fashioned floor lamp and a huge potted plant helped complete the cozy setting. In the audience area, the press jockeyed for position. Jordan took a deep breath. "Ready, Grandma?"

"One moment. I told Blake to get Andrew up here. He can escort us out, then stand to the side. Not only does it put a bodyguard in between us and the cameras, it adds another layer to the boyfriend story."

Andrew came through a service door adjusting his tie. Besides handsome, he looked intimidating in a Secret Service way.

Jordan reached up and straightened the tie. "If I knew you looked this good in a suit, I would have had you wear one on the job."

Andrew raised a brow.

"Stop flirting, you two." Grandma shook her head. "Andrew, give me your arm. It suits me to look every second of my eighty-five years this afternoon and appear to need help. The press is not as calm as I would like."

Jordan followed them through the service door into the ball-room. Like her grandmother, Jordan sat on the edge of her chair, back straight, facing the center camera. Grandma recited the prepared press statement in a conversational tone, reiterating the tone of the statements given over the years. Jordan concluded with her heartfelt lines. "As always, we wish to remember the families and loved ones of this tragedy and others around the world. Everyone experiences loss. Let us all be kinder to one another."

As soon as the prepared statement had ended, the press showered the two women with questions. Grandma and Jordan held up their hands, simultaneously quieting the press.

"We will entertain a few questions as long as you can respect the solemnity of this moment," said Grandma.

The reporters quieted and raised their hands. Grandma, acting every bit the queen, gestured to one of them.

"Will you hold a special memorial service?"

As planned, Jordan answered the predictable question. "The annual private commemoration for the immediate families will be held for the last time this spring. Memorial services for my parents were held years ago. We will not be repeating them."

The consequent smattering of questions was easily answered by referring the press back to the statement or authorities working on the plane's recovery.

Grandma nodded at Andrew to escort them off stage. As they crossed the room, a bold reporter shouted, "Miss Lee, is he really your boyfriend or a cover so you can date Storm Tordon in secret?"

Jordan kept walking, knowing that any answer she gave them would be overanalyzed. What idiot imagined she would ever date Storm?

Andrew and the rest of the bodyguards spent the evening preparing for Mrs. Lee to return immediately to LA and moving

Jordan into September's rental house without appearing to do so. Andrew, along with one bodyguard, would stay at the Lee's condo and the adjoining one to keep the appearance that the condos were in use. Andrew would have preferred to be closer to Jordan, but living in the same house was too close for Mr. Blake, Claire, and him.

At intervals, he walked around the condo, turning a light on or off. On the list of boring bodyguard jobs, house sitting sat at the top. It had been years since he'd pulled this assignment. His phone played Jordan's song. "Hey."

"Blake left with Grandma on a charter. Blake's wife doesn't want him on field duty yet."

Good call. "What are you doing?"

"Calling you. Wishing you were here to play Oreo checkers."

"Deidre might play if you need a game. She should be off duty."

"I believe she's in her room talking to her boyfriend, so a game of checkers wouldn't have any appeal."

They talked about everything and nothing for a while.

Jordan yawned. "I told Paul I'd be ready to work on the next scene tomorrow. I should go to bed."

"Do you still want to go to Hannah's?"

"I do, but if it snows, we'll be moving filming up to the mansion. I think you need to go talk to her anyway. There is a portfolio in the second dresser drawer that has some signed photos of me. Take her one if I can't go, okay?"

"I will."

"Good night, Andrew."

He made one more round of the condo, turning off the lights. Tomorrow had to be a better day.

DESPITE BITTER-COLD TEMPERATURES, NO SNOW fell during the night. Jordan's Southern California body rebelled at the chill in the air.

Deidre laughed at her as they hurried into the trailer. "A hoodie *and* coat?"

In the trailer, Jordan unwound her scarf. "I can still see my breath! This isn't funny."

"Be glad you have all indoor scenes today."

"Best part is none of them involve Storm. I don't think I could get lost in my character enough to not have to do a dozen takes." Although it wasn't top news, the video release still hurt almost a week later. Mostly because the cleanup involved Andrew and partial lies. Jordan slipped into the bedroom for her first wardrobe change of the day.

During lunch, the long-expected snowflakes made their first appearance of the year. Paul danced around as if he'd never seen the stuff. After checking the weather apps, he declared they would shoot the snow scenes on Saturday. Paul spent the next ten minutes yelling, "It's imperative we get the next two scenes done today."

The scenes were not complicated, and the last one was between Princess Sam and her faithful maid.

"Cut!" yelled Paul for the fourth time. "Suzi, you've played the role of the maid for three years! Take a break and get your mind back in your acting space."

"Sorry, Jordan." Suzi shook out her apron.

"Don't worry, it's probably my fault for running out on this scene yesterday."

Suzi took a bottle of water from the catering table. "When I heard the news, I didn't think you would be filming today."

"I wondered that for a moment myself, but I finished grieving for my parents years ago. I'm very relieved at this point. No more anonymous letters from people saying they've had a psychic vision and my parents are living in Siberia. Besides, I didn't want to film on another Saturday. I guess Mother Nature fixed that."

"Fake snow works. Half the Hearthfire movies have the stuff." Suzi walked off in the direction of makeup.

Nodding to Deidre, Jordan retrieved her phone from Princess's vest. No way would filming wrap up in time for her to go to Hannah's. She sent Andrew a text to go without her. With filming tomorrow, she didn't know when she'd be available for a visit.

What would a nice nine-to-five job be like? Jordan banished the thought as she returned to the set and slipped back into the role of Princess Sam.

Hannah's house stood out on the street as the only one that was wheelchair accessible. Andrew parked in the driveway. He'd added a Princess Sam doll to Jordan's offering of a photo, hoping to ease the preteen's disappointment.

Hannah's mother answered the door. Andrew could see Hannah in the room beyond, so he signed with one hand as he spoke.

"I'm sorry Jordan couldn't make it this afternoon. May I still talk with you about the shooting?"

While the mother looked unsure, Hannah signed yes.

Andrew gave the gifts to Hannah and sat down. "Jordan wanted to be here, but they had some delays at work."

"I saw the TV last night. You were with ..." Hannah made a sign Andrew didn't know. "You are her boyfriend, right?"

Andrew imitated the sign and asked her what it meant.

"Name sign for Jordan Lee."

"Thank you. I didn't know that sign."

"My friends and I made it up." Hannah beamed.

"I think she will like it."

"Why do you sign?"

"It's a beautiful language. I fell in love with it. I used to be an interpreter. And I need ASL from time to time in my work as a bodyguard."

"Okay. What do you want to ask me?"

"My job is to protect Jordan." It was close enough to the truth ,Andrew didn't feel the need to explain. "I was watching a video of an interview and saw you in the background signing to your mom. I'd like to know what you saw that day."

Mother and daughter exchanged looks. "Hannah didn't duck like the rest of us. She told me someone else did the shooting and the police were wrong. But what she says is a little crazy." The mother's voice trailed off. She hadn't bothered to sign.

Andrew signed as he spoke. "My brother and I have been looking at video after video of the shooting. I think the police may have arrested the wrong man."

"Mom, I told you. The man in the purple shirt used the gun and then jumped on the man next to him. The police took the second man away, then everyone congratulated the man in the purple shirt."

Andrew opened his phone and found the photos he'd taken of the Hearthfire bodyguards. The deep burgundy of their uniforms was close enough to purple. "Can you tell me if any of these men is the one you saw?" Andrew scrolled through the photos.

"Stop." Hannah pointed to the photo of Rod.

Hannah's mom chimed in. "That's the man Hannah insists was the shooter. I told her she must be wrong. He's a bodyguard."

Andrew put his phone away. "You have been an enormous help. I'm not the police, but I have been wondering if this man could have been part of things. I think you should call the police and tell them. I have the video with Hannah signing 'wrong man, purple shirt' over and over in the background, so the detective will know you aren't making the story up."

Hannah turned to her mother. "Please, Mom. I need to tell the police."

"She's been asking to talk to the police since this happened. Do you think they will have an interpreter?"

"They should be able to find one." Andrew hoped he was correct.

"Will you stay?" asked Hannah.

"If you want me to."

Andrew checked his phone. Jordan wouldn't get a text until she was done filming. Besides, his contact should be Deidre, not the client. He texted Alan.

I have new information about airport shooting.

—In meeting. Can it wait?

Andrew wanted Alan to take care of things now, but it had already been a month. **Sure, after the meeting is fine.**

He hit send. A police car pulled up. He'd have to wait to text Deidre.

A nagging feeling told him he should text her now. He stared at his screen. No, he was letting his feelings for Jordan cause him to overreact.

There was rarely a need to contact the client in situations like this. Panicky principals were harder to protect. Jordan was on set with Deidre and the team. No wonder Adam quit being September's protection. Love messed with the thought process.

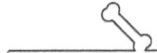

"Miss Lee, Paul wants to film the snow scene up at the mansion tonight." Kittie came into the trailer with a parka and the rest of the wardrobe for the scene.

Jordan took a deep breath. "I thought he was going to shoot day for night."

Kittie shrugged. "I guess he figured he had one chance."

"Thanks, Kittie. I'll be out in a minute."

Jordan waited until Kittie left the trailer to talk to Deidre. "Sorry about this. I didn't know. Trust Paul to make a last-minute change."

"I assume he isn't planning on moving the trailer up there." Deidre leashed Princess. "I'll send her back to the house with someone."

Jordan changed into snow pants and a sweater. She was thinking she needed to send a message to Andrew when someone pounded on the side of the trailer. A cold wind slammed into her as she opened the door.

Kittie waited for her. "The car is over here. Hurry."

Trying to tug on the parka, Jordan followed Kittie to the SUV, where Rod sat in the driver's seat. Jordan climbed in. She didn't even have her seat belt fastened when Rod pulled out of the lot.

"Hey, we need to wait—"

"I was told to get you there as soon as possible." Rod turned onto the highway leading north.

Jordan twisted in her seat to see if another car was following them. "Did Storm already leave?"

"He left a couple hours ago," answered Kittie, handing Jordan her reusable water bottle.

"Thanks." Something was wrong. Jordan took a long drink, then pulled her phone out of her pocket.

Kittie snatched it away.

"Aglet."

"What did you say?" asked Rod.

"Aglet. Kittie broke my aglet." The Hastings app better be listening.

ANDREW DUSTED THE SNOW OFF his windshield before climbing into his car. As soon as his phone connected with the system, he called Deidre, but her phone went straight to voicemail, so he called dispatch.

"Can you put me on with Alan and Deidre?"

"They're already on a call. Can you hold a minute?"

"Tell them I have critical information."

"One minute."

Andrew eased onto the street and headed for September's rental.

"Connecting you to the call. Deidre, Alan, Adam, and Liam Dermot are already on."

Why so many?

"This is Alan. Are you driving?"

"Yes."

"Pull over."

Andrew pulled into an empty elementary-school parking lot. "I'm parked. What's wrong?"

"Jordan is missing." Deidre's voice exuded a practiced calm.

"Do you know where Rod is?"

"What?" asked several voices.

209

"Hannah, the deaf girl in the video, identified Rod as the shooter. She just reported it to the police." If slamming his head on the steering wheel would help, he would do it. If only he'd gone with his gut and texted Deidre.

"How long have you known this?" asked Adam.

"About an hour. I told Hannah I'd stay with her while she talked to the police. I knew Jordan was on set, so I didn't call."

When no one said anything, Andrew's frustration mounted.

Deidre's voice came over the phone. "My team talked with Stu and Paul, who are back at the hotel. Rod had the afternoon off. And Kittie must be involved. She came in with some wardrobe items and told Jordan that Paul wanted to film up at the mansion. Paul says he has no intention of shooting tonight."

"Do you think they are going to the mansion?" Andrew checked the system for Jordan's phone. "Last known location was on the highway heading to the mansion fifteen minutes ago."

"The team is already heading there." Deidre's voice remained calm.

It took all his willpower to not yell at Deidre for letting Jordan out of her sight.

Andrew started his car. "I'm en route too."

"Andrew, you are to go back to the house." Adam's voice held as much authority as their father's.

"No. If I had told Alan this couldn't wait, Deidre would have known Jordan wasn't safe on the set."

"I've contacted the police." It took Andrew a moment to place the voice as Liam's. "The mansion is outside their jurisdiction, and they are transferring me to the sheriff. Do you know what vehicle they might be in?"

Deidre rattled off the information. Andrew checked his GPS and pulled out of the parking lot.

"Andrew." Adam's stern voice echoed throughout the car. "At least wait for backup before you go rushing in."

"I will unless I can't."

Jordan didn't drink more of the water, fearing they might have drugged it. Rod tossed her phone out the window, and Kittie pulled out a set of zip ties. "We can tie you up, or you can play nice. Either way, I will blindfold you now."

The zip ties were probably not the ones from props guaranteed to break if she brought her hands down fast and hit her thigh. "I'll cooperate."

Jordan prayed as Kitty tied a familiar blue scarf around Jordan's eyes.

Andrew turned off the highway at the exit for the mansion. He recognized an SUV at the side of the road as one of the Dermot vehicles.

"Deidre, I see one of your team vehicles. Have they recovered the phone?" Andrew didn't stop to confer with the bodyguards.

"Yes. As assumed, it's useless. I'm a minute behind you. Wait at the gas station. The map I have shows multiple points of entry to the property. I want a plan going in."

Having calmed down significantly, Andrew pulled off. "I'm waiting. Just make me part of the team."

"We need to be clear on one thing. I'm in charge, not you." Deidre pulled up behind Andrew. "Jordan is my principal, not yours."

"Agreed."

A couple of grunts, most likely belonging to Alan and Adam, echoed through the line.

"Alan, Adam, and Liam." No softness remained in Deidre's voice. "Please mute yourselves. I need you as support. Andrew agreed I'm lead. I don't need you undermining him. Andrew, get out of that car, and let's get a plan in place."

Andrew wasted no time following Deidre's orders.

Jordan wasn't exactly sure they were in the mansion. The turns and stairs weren't familiar to her. She was shoved to her knees. A door slammed. Jordan waited a few moments, then, sensing she was alone, cautiously removed her blindfold.

Through the windows overlooking the property, she could see the snow silently filling the yard. Jordan recognized the tree line from when they had filmed the wolf scene. She was in a room at the north end of the mansion on the second floor.

She looked around the room for a door only to discover there wasn't one. But how could that be? She'd heard one close. With the window, it wasn't meant to be a secret room, more like an escape room. She'd solved escape-room scenarios before, and though most of them had been according to script, it couldn't be that difficult.

Headlights flashed across the window. Had Andrew gotten her message? She looked outside to see a red sports car. Storm? He was staying on the property. He would be the least likely to rescue her. Maybe he'd come to investigate. She pressed closer to the window, wondering if the dim light of the room was enough to alert him to her presence. The car drove around to the front of the house.

Storm could be using Rod and Kittie as his minions, not that she'd ever seen him talk to either of them with anything other than passing acquaintance. As eager as Kittie was to make a name in Hollywood, she might listen to Storm, but why Rod?

Starting at the picture windows, Jordan circled the room, running her fingers along chair railings and scanning the wooden panels. The second panel from the left on the back wall had a seam running along the left side. Jordan searched for a way to turn the overhead light off, hoping to see light through a crack, but there wasn't a light switch either.

Thanks to Blake's training, she found a hidden camera no bigger than a pea between the brass bookend and a pristine copy of the works of Robert Louis Stevenson. There had to be others. Disabling them would only use up her time. If someone was watching her, appearing to bumble around might entertain them and give her more time—time for Deidre and Andrew to find her. The bookshelf made an obvious trap door. They'd used them in at least two episodes of Princess Sam. Jordan lifted the bookends and pulled out the larger books, which were arranged in no order that she could determine. Classics next to little-known authors, nonfiction next to fantasy. She felt along the shelving. Nothing.

Jordan sat down behind the desk. It faced the panel she'd identified as a possible door. Her fingers explored the edge of the desk until they hit something smooth and round. Could it be that easy? She pushed the button, and the panel slid open. Storm stood in the doorway.

Andrew checked the clock on the dash. It had been forty minutes since Jordan's use of aglet-initiated emergency protocols. Thirty since her phone had gone silent.

Deidre's team used all three cars to cover the entrances to the mansion. No one joined Andrew in his. The snow became their friend as any side roads without tracks were quickly eliminated.

Andrew turned off at the entrance to the cottage Storm was using. He turned off the headlights and inched along the tree-lined lane. His car would only be hidden while in the shadows along the snow-covered road.

A black square of pavement marked the spot where Storm's red sports car usually sat. Tire tracks marked the road up to the main mansion. Andrew followed them.

Rod pushed Storm into the room and leveled a gun at both of them. "Miss Lee, it's unfortunate you found the way out so quickly. I gotta disable this door. Storm, I got her alone like you asked."

Storm held up his hands. "Not like this, man. This isn't what I meant when I said I wanted a moment alone with her."

"No, I suppose not. You prefer to seduce your victims. No clear-cut #metoo moments. Always consensual. Making promises you never keep. You didn't even like Kittie, did you? Even though she is still stupid enough to believe herself in love with you. Miss backup date of the year. That's my twin sister you've been leading along and warming your nights with. And it all ends tonight." He pointed the gun at Jordan's head. "The world will mourn Hollywood's cutest orphan one last time. What about the rest of us? You missed us!" Rod yanked Kittie to his side.

Storm glanced back at Jordan, his expression mirroring her confusion.

Keep them talking. The advice from the show in the second season where Princess Sam was kidnapped came to mind. "What are you talking about? How did we miss you?"

"You and your grandmother with all your fancy memorials and gifts and scholarships. You forgot us!" Rod's face burned with rage.

Figuring she had a better chance if she wasn't sitting, Jordan stood. She'd memorized the family lists from the crash years ago. Rod and Kittie were not on the list. "How did we miss you?"

"The charter company your father rented the plane from for his humanitarian mission went under. Did you know that?"

"How could I? I could barely read at the time. I knew it wasn't around anymore, but a lot of things aren't." Jordan stealthily moved to the corner of the desk beneath the window.

"Our father owned the company. All he had left was his life insurance and a small commuter plane. He ran that plane into the ground hoping Kittie and I would have something while you, the precious child actress, danced across film after film. Never knowing hunger or the embarrassment of having a checker look down on your mother as she used food stamps to pay for our groceries."

Jordan held a hand up in a calming gesture. "Rod, Kittie, I didn't know. I didn't realize."

"Oh, shut up." Rod trained the gun at Storm. "You have ten minutes with her. Then it's our turn."

The door slid shut. Jordan reached for the button, but the door didn't move.

Storm took a step toward her. "Jordan, this is not what I asked for. He's psycho."

"What did you ask for?"

"I paid them $500 to get me alone with you." As impossible as it was, Storm managed to lower her opinion of him.

"I suggest we find a way out. You've been in more action movies than I have. What would your characters do?"

"Break the window, kiss the girl, and jump to safety."

Jordan grabbed a brass bookend and hurled it at the window, but it bounced off and fell to the floor.

"Throw it harder, like this." Storm picked up another bookend, smashing it into the window. Bugs did more damage to a car's windshield than Storm did with the bookend.

"Next idea?"

"I'm only an actor. I don't know. Yell for help?" Storm pounded on the window with his fist.

The room lights went out. Jordan peered out the window, trying to see if there were any lights other than the moon reflected in the snow. The lights lining the driveway were also out. "Stop pounding for a moment. The door you came in used an electric opener. I think the power is out. Let's see if we can pry it open. Use the bookend."

Storm fumbled his way across the room. Jordan moved slowly along the wall, searching for another exit, the oriental rug snagging on her foot as she went. The clang of metal rang through the room as Storm pounded on the door.

"It's no use. The door is made of steel. And it's warm."

"What do you mean warm?"

"I smell smoke!"

Jordan crossed the room to the door and Storm. He was right, the door was warm, and the smell of smoke was growing stronger. "Do you have your phone?"

"No, Rod took it from me."

Jordan's list of unasked questions was growing. A flash of light came through the window. Two dark SUVs drove up the drive. "Storm, I think it is my bodyguards."

"We're saved?"

"Not if they can't find us. Let's work on breaking the window."

"Won't that make the fire worse? It does in my movies." Any other time, Storm's perplexed look would have been amusing.

"The mansion is on fire! I'm going in!" Andrew yelled at his phone.

"Wait, I can see the house. Don't do this alone!"

Deidre couldn't see the flames on the second floor from the side she was coming from. Andrew leaped out of the car, bypassing the front door and running to the corner, where a smaller door stood. Stu had shown him the fire riser on their tour. The doorknob turned but didn't open. Andrew yanked on the nob again. Someone had moved a large rock in front of the door. Andrew pushed it out of the way and tore open the door. It only took a second to find the right lever and hopefully send water through the fire-sprinkler system.

As Andrew turned to run into the house, a shadowy figure rose in front of him, swinging something at his head. Andrew ducked a second too late and the blow connected with his head. He lunged for the person and heard a shot fired. Pain ripped through Andrew's side as his head hit the pavement and the snowy world dissolved into darkness.

Fire alarms sounded, and water poured from the ceiling's fire-sprinkler system.

Jordan pushed the damp hair out of her face. "Unlike a movie, the water works. But we still need to find a way out."

As Storm kept pushing at the window, Jordan surveyed the room on the off chance that Rod hadn't lied about a second way out. Her eye caught on the rug that had lifted where she had tripped over it. She knelt and pulled up the corner of the rug. "Storm, I found a trapdoor."

Storm stopped his pounding and dropped to his knees next to Jordan. Together they pulled on the ring attached to the top. The door didn't budge. "Help me move the carpet back."

Storm rolled the rug toward the center of the room. "There's some sort of hole in the wood here—not a knothole, more like a puzzle piece. It's like the giant keyhole in *Adventures of the Zombie Tomb Raider*. We need a key. Something big. At least the size of the palm of my hand."

Jordan felt the irregular edges of the hole. "The bookend?"

Storm tried it several ways. "There has got to be something else close in size."

Jordan tried to look around, but the constantly spraying water made it difficult to see. "I saw a small statue on a shelf earlier."

They slid over the water-soaked floor to the bookshelf wall. Red-and-blue lights flashed through the window. Jordan ran her hands over books searching for the statue.

"I got it!" Storm rushed over to the hole, which was now filling with water. He shoved the statue in, and the trapdoor sprung open.

An EMT applied pressure to Andrew's side as another applied pressure to his head.

"Jordan? Where's Jordan?" Andrew tried to push himself up only to find he was strapped to a gurney.

"We have your guys, and the fire department and the police here. They'll find her. You already played the hero for one night."

Deidre appeared at his feet. "Is he going to be okay?"

"Yes, ma'am."

"I'm here, you know." Andrew tried to get up again.

"I don't know if I should yell at you or thank you. I told you to wait. But you got the fire sprinklers started and took down one of the two perps while getting shot. I've had your brothers and Liam yelling in my ear for the last ten minutes."

"Where's Jordan?"

"They're still looking for her."

"Why aren't you doing anything?"

"The police and fire departments are following protocol. You know we have to stay out of their way." Deidre paused for a moment and rolled her eyes. "Can you three stop yelling? I'm going to take this earpiece out, stomp on it, and bury it in the snow."

The EMT cast Deidre an odd look.

"Adam is furious and wants me to fire you on the spot. Alan isn't so sure, and your dad just joined the conversation."

Andrew reached a hand out. "Let me talk to them."

Deidre pulled her phone out of her pocket and pushed a button. "You guys are on speakerphone, and there's an audience."

"Dad, don't fire Deidre. I didn't listen."

"Good to hear the bullet knocked some sense into you."

A voice he didn't recognize broke in. "The fire is contained. They are searching the house now."

"There are secret passages. Jordan could be in there."

"What?" several voices asked over the phone.

"Alan do you have a floor plan on your computer? The only entrance Stu showed me was …" Andrew struggled to find the words.

The EMT turned to the monitors. "We need to get him to the hospital."

Deidre grabbed her phone and disappeared.

Another cobweb hit Jordan in the face. Smoke permeated the corridor. She held her soggy blue scarf over her mouth and nose.

"I don't think anyone has been in here for years." Storm's voice came from behind her.

"Real spiderwebs feel much grosser than props."

"Hey, I think I found something."

Jordan took a step back, feeling for what she had missed when she'd run into the last cobweb.

Storm grunted and pushed, and the wall of the passage swung out revealing the grand ballroom.

A shout came from the other end of the room. Several firemen rushed over, then led them outside. Someone threw a blanket around Jordan's shoulders and ushered her into the ambulance behind Storm.

"Do you know if there was anyone else in there?" asked a police officer.

"Rod and Kittie locked us in a room." Jordan coughed as an EMT checked her vitals.

"Just a man and a woman?"

"They're the only ones I saw. Rod is a bodyguard for Hearthfire." Jordan coughed again. "Kittie is part of the studio crew." Someone held an oxygen mask to her face.

"How did you get out?" asked the officer.

Storm coughed before answering. "Secret passage. Rarely can I play the hero in real life."

Jordan rolled her eyes. *Save it for the paparazzi.*

The EMT put an oxygen mask on Storm and made him lie back on the stretcher. "Can we get these two to the hospital?"

The officer nodded. "We can ask the rest of our questions later."

Deidre appeared behind the officer, but they were already closing the ambulance doors. Jordan went to pull the mask away from her face, but the EMT stopped her. "Just lie back and breathe."

As she breathed in the rubbery-plastic smell of the mask, two questions ran through her mind. What exactly did Storm have to do with this, and where was Andrew?

The ambulance driver hit another bump. Between the pain and occasional question from one of the EMTs, Andrew lay analyzing everything that had gone wrong. Everything *he* had caused to go wrong. If only he'd listened to Adam. Bottom line, if he'd followed his gut and called Deidre, Rod wouldn't have kidnapped Jordan.

Who was he kidding, anyway? A bodyguard falling for his principal was a recipe for disaster. Mr. Blake, Claire Lee, and the entire family had warned him. If Jordan had died because of him … Andrew pushed that possibility out of his mind. If they both lived through this, he would let her go.

The EMT's voice floated above him. Andrew tried to process what he was saying. The EMT tried again. "Everyone is out and alive."

Andrew closed his eyes and thanked God his actions hadn't killed Jordan.

"I'm fine, Grandma. Really. Just a little smoke and about eight broken fingernails." Jordan sat in a hospital room that resembled exactly the one she'd been in a month before.

"Paul says they're closing down and finishing up at the studio here in LA since we can no longer use the mansion. Otherwise I'd be on the first plane out of here, even if Blake forbids it." Grandma would have hired the plane too.

"I heard the same thing. I'll be home sometime tomorrow. I'll take the first plane I can get."

"I just don't understand how this could have happened." Claire's voice got loud enough that Jordan had to pull the phone away from her ear. "I thought that bodyguard of yours loved you. How did he let you get hurt?"

"Andrew didn't let me get hurt. Remember, we fired him. He wasn't even working on my detail. But he still tried to come save me and is in surgery now." Jordan swallowed the tears that threatened.

"That isn't what I heard."

"Grandma, I love you, and I'm not up to arguing with you. It has been a long day. I will be home sometime tomorrow." Jordan ended the call and set the phone on silent. She didn't need anyone else calling her asking questions. The police had already taken her statement. Deidre had been allowed to sit in, so Jordan wouldn't need to repeat the story.

Blaming Deidre was as ridiculous as blaming Andrew. Not for a moment had she suspected Kittie's involvement. Jordan knew the moment she saw Rod that something was off. If she'd waited for Deidre or Stu it wouldn't have happened. She trusted Kittie, who had been with the crew for two years, Rod with Hearthfire almost as long. No one had seen it coming. Twins? One of them must have changed names.

Deidre tapped on the door and let herself in. "Andrew is out of surgery. He lost enough blood they had to give him a transfusion. They are going to keep him in ICU tonight. You can see him in the morning."

"Do you have any more news?"

Deidre sat down in the bedside chair. "A twist none of us saw coming. Kittie was the one who fired the gun as Rod was attacking Andrew. She claims she didn't mean to hit Andrew. I'm unclear, but something happened when they set the fire. They argued. As you probably guessed, Kittie has a huge crush on Storm, so she didn't want Rod to turn off the fire sprinklers. One of my guards watched her arrest. She was screaming up a storm, claiming she'd arranged the airport shooting and Rod was too stupid to plan anything."

"How does that work with Hannah's story?"

"I'm not sure. We might never know. Rod didn't make it. But even if she was the one who arranged it, Rod still could have pulled the trigger."

"He's dead?"

Deidre nodded. "As near as I can figure, Storm had asked Rod and Kittie to get you up to the mansion for a romantic rendezvous. Suzi was in on it, trying to keep you on the set late enough that most everyone else would have left. Storm tried to get Kittie to help him weeks ago. Long story short, Kittie found the video on his phone and was the one who released it. Or, rather, got Reggie to, hoping to end your career. Apparently, Reggie tried out for some of the same roles you did for next year."

"Reggie? I thought we were friends." Friendship didn't matter when it came to being cast for the next role.

Deidre took a sip of her water. "Back to today. Storm didn't know that Rod had his own issues or that Kittie was Rod's twin sister. He claims he just wanted to talk to you alone. It's unclear what they had planned for you after Storm left. Rod used a lighter on the wall hanging. It burned faster than he intended and the wallpaper caught on fire. Kittie wasn't clear on what happened next other than he slapped her. The fire marshal still needs to investigate."

"Please tell me something that doesn't sound like my life is being written by a washed-up soap-opera scriptwriter."

Deidre smiled a half smile. "I hadn't thought of it like that. Storm sends his apologies. After talking with him, I do think he really does want to date you, even though he is a bit misguided on the term *date*. His plan was just to have you up for dinner so the two of you could talk. I think he believes that's all it would have taken for you to succumb to his charms."

"Not happening."

"Get some sleep. I'll have someone outside all night."

"Thanks, Deidre. Let me know when I can see Andrew?"

Deidre nodded and left.

Jordan adjusted her hospital gown. She really was trapped in a soap opera.

Familiar voices woke Andrew. "Mom? Dad?"

"Good morning. How are you feeling?" Mom's voice broke through the fog in Andrew's head.

"Mildly drugged, like there should be more pain." Andrew felt for his side.

"Doctor says you are lucky. The bullet grazed your liver." Dad stood at the foot of the bed. "You also took a nasty hit to the head."

"They want to keep you in for another day or two." Mom patted his hand.

"How's Jordan?"

Mom looked at Dad before answering. "She left you a letter. They let her come in yesterday before she flew back to California."

Andrew processed the words. "What day is it?"

"Sunday." His parents answered in unison

"What happened to Saturday?"

"You reacted to the pain meds and were hallucinating, so they sedated you to keep you from harming yourself." Dad's face hinted at a smile. "You thought there was a dragon in the room."

Andrew closed his eyes. "Did I embarrass myself as badly as I did when I had my tonsils out?"

"You didn't propose to anyone, if that's what you mean," said Mom.

"However, the nurses have nicknamed you Sir Andrew." Dad chuckled.

A nurse tapped on the door. "Glad to see you're back with us." She proceeded to check Andrew's vitals and bandages. "I'll let the doctor know you're awake. I know you are hungry. Start with the ice chips, and you can work up to other foods. With your stitches, we don't want you eating something you aren't ready for." After making a note in the computer, she left.

Andrew took a deep breath. Ouch! He took another because he deserved the pain. "If I had followed my gut, it wouldn't have happened."

"Maybe, maybe not." Mom smoothed his sheets. "The detective was pretty skeptical of Hannah's story. Rod would have tried again. The news that the plane crash may have been mechanical error that unhinged Rod, thinking that everyone would blame his father."

"Why?"

"His father owned the charter plane. Rod's twin sister, Kittie, used his anger to fuel her revenge. She felt that Jordan and Claire Lee owed her a chance to make it big. Claire Lee didn't know either of them was related to anyone that had to do with the plane. Kittie's been ranting to the police. She claims she didn't mean to shoot you."

"Kittie shot me?"

"More like you got hit when she was trying to kill her brother for starting the fire and trying to kill Storm." Mom shook her head.

"I know I'm in for a huge lecture. Can you get it over with now while I'm still on pain meds?"

Dad shook his head. "There isn't much of one to give. Deidre, Adam, and I have been over things. Even if you had gotten your warning about Rod to Deidre, she wouldn't have suspected Kittie of lying about shooting the snow scene up at the mansion. Paul was desperate for snow. Had Jordan known Rod was a possible suspect, she probably would have put up a struggle before leaving the lot. Then she might have been injured. The only change is Jordan would not have been left alone on the lot, even for the couple of minutes it took for Deidre to hand the dog over."

She shouldn't have been left alone anyway. Andrew knew better than to voice his thoughts.

"Before you go blaming Deidre, Stu was outside the trailer when she left with Princess. Only the driver and Deidre had been allowed to stay at the studio. You got on the call with everyone else within two minutes of realizing what happened. I'd say your only mistake was going off on your own, except you got the fire-suppression system started, which probably saved Jordan and Storm's lives, giving them time to get out of the room they were trapped in. Deidre didn't know about the fire riser or the secret passages. No lecture."

"This story sounds too bizarre. Are you sure I'm not still hallucinating?" Andrew rolled onto his left side, searching for a more comfortable position.

Mom adjusted his pillows. "On her way out, Jordan joked about her life being written by an unemployed soap-opera scriptwriter."

"May I have her letter?"

Mom handed him the envelope. "We'll go call your siblings."

Andrew opened the get-well-soon card. The illustration was of a dog resembling Princess.

Andrew,

I wish I could have talked to you before I left. I'm sorry you got shot. Most actors go through their entire life without a bodyguard getting injured, and I get two shot in a month. I've gone back to LA, but you probably know that.

I'll miss you. Call soon.

Jordan

Andrew's heart sunk. He'd hoped for more. Even a heart or a paw print. Maybe she had come to the same conclusion he had. While sweet, their romance was doomed. She'd been right to dump him when she had. At least this way it could fade into a nice memory. No tearful breakup or commitments to just be friends. He tucked the card back into the envelope and closed his eyes, hoping he really was dreaming.

MARIA APPLIED THE LAST OF Jordan's makeup. "I've done all I can do, but I can't pull that sadness out of your eyes."

"Maybe you can emphasize my scar?" Jordan lifted her hair, searching for the scar from last month's shooting.

"Sorry, the plastic surgeon did too good of a job when he patched you up. Don't frown like that. Most actresses would be pleased."

"I'm just not looking forward to this on-set interview. I know why Hearthfire needs us to do it, but I'm not ready."

"I don't know that any of us are. I wanted to slap Reggie when I did her makeup earlier." Maria gathered up her brushes.

"Really? With everything that has happened, I think the video is the least of my worries."

"Five minutes, Miss Lee." The new tech person looked up from her tablet.

Blake moved from his post near the door, tilted his head, and signed "Go." Jordan checked her phone one last time before handing it over to him. Three days and still no word from Andrew. If something had happened to him, Jethro Hastings would have called Blake.

Taking a cleansing breath, Jordan stepped onto the set for the castle parlor. Paul, Storm, Reggie, and Suzi already sat in their seats, along with Jet James, the anchor for the entertainment news show. Jordan took the only seat left on the couch next to Storm. Near the camera stood three of Hearthfire's top executives, sending the clear message that this interview was important to them.

Jet raised her microphone. Before she could speak, one executive stepped forward. "Just a reminder: Rod's and Kittie's roles in the incident are to be referred to as 'alleged.' We are not a criminal court. Ms. James, our lawyers have the right to pull sections of this interview they feel would impede the criminal investigations, so please tread lightly on those subjects."

Jet raised her microphone again, then faced the camera. "I'm here tonight with the cast and director of *Adventures of Princess Sam*. In recent weeks, the final show has been plagued with accidents, rumors, and real-life adventures. Let's start our first question with the director. Everyone wants to know—will the Christmas special air as planned?"

"Yes. Despite the obstacles we've faced, we have a remarkable cast and crew and are very close to finishing on schedule." Paul didn't mention that some of the remaining scenes were being modified or written out.

Jordan smiled and concentrated on not rolling her eyes as Reggie delivered a tear-filled apology for betraying Storm and Jordan by releasing the kiss video. Beside her, Storm tensed as Jet moved to him. "Why did you make that video?"

"I wanted to analyze Jordan's acting skills. We'd had a bit of an argument. I must say I'm impressed. Even I bought that the kiss with the bodyguard was real."

"Jordan, you were asked last week if your so-called dating of this bodyguard was just a ruse. At the time, you didn't answer. I notice he's not here. Do you have an answer now?"

Has it only been a week? It seemed like a lifetime ago.

"Jet, as you have most likely heard, Andrew is recovering from a gunshot wound sustained while protecting me. We were not dating at the time Storm recorded the video. However, we have since formed a bond."

Andrew recognized Jordan's princess persona even through the TV.

"Are you dating?"

Jordan smiled the same secretive smile her grandmother had used in an early seventies romantic comedy Andrew watched last night. "Jet, you should know a princess never kisses and tells."

What kind of answer was that? Safe. Andrew reached for the remote. He'd been giving his family the same type of answer. None. It wasn't like he could borrow his brother-in-law's airplane and fly to LA. Even if the plane did have a bed. And what would be the point? To deliver some grand, "I'm sorry it didn't work out" speech?

No, it was better to let their relationship die like the melting snow.

"THAT'S A WRAP!" PAUL'S ANNOUNCEMENT of two hours ago echoed through Jordan's mind. Two weeks after arriving back in LA, she was done playing the role of princess forever. And they'd finished on Friday to avoid one of Paul's ill-tempered Saturday sessions.

The filming ended up being more rather than less of what was planned. Kittie had been an extra in several of the scenes, including the wedding kiss, and so Paul had forced them to reshoot the scene. To Jordan's surprise, Storm played a perfect gentleman on and off screen. And Jordan didn't contradict his claims that he'd saved them; after all, Storm had located the key to the exit tunnel.

Jordan hugged Maria and left an envelope with a gift card where Maria was sure to find it. Her goodbyes to the rest of the cast and crew were short. For the first time in years, Jordan wouldn't be back on the lot next week. Her Hearthfire contract was complete.

She checked her dressing room for any personal items one last time. The ball Andrew bought for Princess sat in the corner. Leaving it there, she turned off the light. "Take me home, Blake."

The driver had pulled the car up to the studio exit. Blake held the back door open with his good arm. He'd ditched the sling earlier in the week. An extra bodyguard sat in the front seat. Blake sat next to her in the back. "Your grandmother would like you to visit her."

"I'll call her later. I need to go home." The few hundred yards between Claire's mansion and Jordan's cottage was only a separation by mutual agreement. If Grandma wanted to see Jordan, nothing could prevent it. But not tonight. Tonight was for chick flicks and ice cream. At least if someone wrote a script, that was what would be in it—a way to mourn the two weeks of silence.

Adam didn't bother knocking before walking into Andrew's apartment. "I see you are still in the same position you were last week. Is that the same shirt? Please tell me you've at least showered."

Andrew glared. "Did Mom talk you into coming?"

"Nope." Adam turned off the TV. "September did."

"I haven't even talked to her."

"Apparently she isn't the only one you haven't talked to." Adam pulled the coffee table over and sat down inches from Andrew. "She says you haven't called Jordan since getting shot. Two weeks. What are you thinking?"

"Thirteen days if you don't count the day they sedated me."

Adam ran his hand down his face. "I know you like to make your own mistakes and not repeat ours, but this one is stupid. For one, you are moping around here instead of being in PT. And don't tell me for a moment you couldn't be working on some desk things. You are the best planner we have. And two, you are going to let love walk away or just hide from it."

"Look, I'm not making the same mistake you did." Andrew lowered the footrest on the recliner. "It wasn't love. She needed me to fool the press. To feel safe. Do you want to read the note she left? You heard her on TV. Besides, I'm going to resign from Hastings as soon as I can. I wasn't meant to be in the family business."

Adam jumped up and paced to the other end of the room. "Little brother, I have never wanted to punch some sense into you before, but right now I wish I could. I saw you with Jordan before the video became public. I saw how much you cared. Dad's been over this with you. It. Wasn't. Your. Fault. But what you are doing right now is. Stop lying to yourself."

Andrew stood, ignoring the dull ache in his side. "Go ahead throw a punch. It will make us both feel better. Or would you rather keep telling me you told me so? My entire life, 'I told you so' is all I have heard from everyone."

"This is messed up, bro. I only came to tell you to call Jordan, not pick a fight. We are all worried about you. None of us has been injured working this job like you have. When Deidre told us you'd been shot..." Adam shook his head. "It was as bad as when September told me what happened to her. Mom and Dad told us not to come up to the hospital. We had to make sure things kept running and our other clients were covered. Between Alan and me, we had to buy a new Mortimer, the punching dummy for the gym. Abbie damaged hers as well, with Alex's help. We all love you. Don't you get it?"

Andrew ignored the moisture he saw in Adam's eyes. "So what? Now you are all going to gang up on me?"

"Abbie volunteered the jet if we came and put you on it."

"Of course she did. She's been bailing me out my entire life."

"No, she's been treating you like a sister does, like your guardian angel. We have always been a team, and we will never leave you behind."

"I'm surprised she isn't here now."

"She's in the car."

For the first time in two weeks, Andrew laughed. "Get her in here. I need some sisterly advice."

Compared to the weeks in Wisconsin, the first of November in California felt like summer. Jordan joined Grandma on her back porch for breakfast.

"How often did you not have a next project lined up?"

"At your age?" Grandma sliced her strawberry into neat circles. "I took a year off to have your father, nurse him, and get back in shape. They didn't have very good pumps then, and I wanted to promote breast-feeding, so working even six hours on a set wasn't feasible."

"Donetta keeps sending over offers. I don't know what to try out for next. Sometimes I feel like my entire life has been one role after another."

"Do you regret that?"

"No, you kept me in line, prevented me from becoming a child-actor statistic. You and Blake were honest about the dangers. Even if I hated your involvement, I knew you were right. Looking back, I know you gave up part of your career to oversee mine." Her dog jumped into her lap.

"I didn't give it up. I made a choice. Yes, I could have hung on to a few parts and cameos, but making sure you knew you were never alone was better."

"And I got my homework done." Jordan rolled her eyes.

"You could go into semiretirement for a while."

"Coming back out is hard. I've watched others try. There are a couple projects that don't start filming until spring. I'm looking at those." She rubbed Princess's belly.

"What will you do in the meantime?"

"September has invited me out to Chicago."

Grandma dropped her fork. "Haven't you been hurt enough?"

"I thought we might have had something real. I hoped to talk with Andrew before I left. I didn't write a very clear note. I owe it to myself to make sure there is no misunderstanding. I hate the romance movies that make you want to yell at the couple to talk."

"Especially the ones you're in?"

"Or the one you filmed in Paris in '62."

They both laughed.

"When do you leave?"

"I have a ticket to O'Hare this afternoon. Blake is sending someone else with me. I figured Princess could stay with you."

Grandma reached over and pulled Jordan into a half hug. "That's my girl."

Andrew stared at Abbie's camera. "I really have to do this?"

"Yes. I don't want you to blame me later."

"Fine. Hit record." Andrew smiled into the camera phone. "I, Andrew Hastings—"

"Andrew David—" prompted Abbie.

"I, Andrew David Hastings, do solemnly swear on this partially sunny first Saturday of November, that I'm getting on this plane of my own free will, that Abbie didn't bribe me beyond offering me the use of the most comfortable jet in the world and my favorite hamburger—"

"You aren't supposed to include the hamburger."

"That I'm going to LA to talk with Jordan Lee and tell her of my undying love for her not because any of my brothers threatened to beat me up but because it is my only wish."

Abbie started laughing. "Cut the dramatics."

"Fine. I'm going because Abbie is right. I can't fix this with a phone call. Abbie is always right, and I'm lucky to have the best sister in the world."

"At least you got that part right." Abbie turned her phone to face her. "Let it be known beyond my generous gift of flight and the aforementioned hamburger that I'm not financing this trip in any other way. There are no strings attached, and Andrew will be welcome at my home whether or not his quest to find true love is fulfilled."

"Oh, now who is being dramatic?"

Abbie turned the phone back to Andrew. "Wave to Mom and Dad and get on the plane. I'll wait until you are gone to send the video to them."

Andrew waved and boarded the plane. "Wish me luck!"

SEPTEMBER OPENED HER FRONT DOOR and laughed. "Oh, Jordan, I'm sorry."

Jordan's bodyguard stayed outside as Jordan followed September into the living room. "What's wrong?"

Adam stood near the TV bouncing Harmony in his arms. "You didn't get the message, did you?"

"What message?"

"The vid—" September bent over, laughing.

"I'm not sure it's that funny." Adam smiled. Harmony laughed, pointing at her mother and clapping her hands. "Sit down, Jordan, and watch this home movie my sister sent my parents early this afternoon. We just got it a half hour ago."

Adam clicked the remote, and the large screen filled with a video of Andrew standing at the bottom of the stairs to a small jet.

The video ended with the plane taking off.

"So where is he now?"

September regained control of her laughter. "According to the Hastings app, he's parked at Claire Lee's. We have been trying to call him. As we agreed, I told no one you were coming. Adam knew it was a possibility Andrew would fly out, but he didn't tell me. I died when he showed me the video."

"So Andrew is at my grandma's, probably being interrogated while we speak?"

September started laughing again. "I could write a country song about this and it would be a number-one hit."

Jordan laughed too. "Can I see it again? I want to hear the part about true love."

"This is the most mixed-up love story since O'Henry's *Gift of the Magi*, and I should know—I've been in two adaptations." Claire handed back Andrew's phone.

"Will you tell me where Jordan is now?" Andrew looked at Mr. Blake, then at the actress.

"Chicago." Mr. Blake laughed.

"Her friend September invited her to come visit. She left this morning and should've landed an hour ago." Claire delivered the explanation with a straight face while Mr. Blake turned away to hide his laughter.

"You're telling me I flew out here to see her and she went to Chicago to see me?" Andrew scratched Princess behind the ears.

Mr. Blake laughed so hard he couldn't answer.

Claire motioned for Andrew to follow her down the hall to a tidy office. "Call her. You're welcome to stay here until she returns." She put a hand on his cheek. "You look as though you need a pain reliever and some sleep."

Andrew sat down in an upholstered chair and opened his phone. Princess jumped in his lap. Perhaps he shouldn't have ignored Adam's calls since he landed at the airport. He only waited for one ring for Jordan to answer.

"September won't stop laughing. Let me go into another room." Muffled sounds filled the next several seconds, then he could hear the sound of a door shutting. "I saw your video."

"The one Abbie recorded?"

"Yes. You've lost some weight."

Andrew rubbed the back of his neck. "Just a little."

"Did you really fly out there to declare your undying love to me?"

"Not in those exact words. But, ya. I didn't want to do it on the phone."

"I have a ticket on the first flight out in the morning. Will you stay there until I get there? Don't bother with a hotel. You can stay at my place."

"Your grandma already said I could stay here. Princess seems to want me to stay too. Claire also told me to take some pain reliever."

"Are you in pain?"

Andrew took a deep breath. "Some. It still hurts to laugh, so I have been trying not to ever since Mr. Blake nearly busted a gut over our situation."

Jordan giggled. "It is pretty funny."

"I love you."

"What?"

"I said I love you. I wanted to say it to your face, but I can't wait any longer."

"I love you too, Andrew. Go get some sleep. Tomorrow you can tell me again and I can kiss you and make everything all better."

Epilogue

JORDAN AND ANDREW WELCOMED HANNAH and her mother to the ASL premier of Princess Sam's Christmas special and posed for photos next to a cutout of Princess Sam.

The idea for shadow signing the end of the series had sprouted during the weekend of their reunion. Soon they'd recruited several deaf actors and started their practices. Jordan would sign her own parts. Andrew took on Storm's roll. A closed-captioned version of the special would be played on a screen hung over the signers' heads as acting out the scenes wasn't feasible. With Hearthfire's agreement to allow the screening, Jordan funded the event herself.

Jordan's signing improved over the month of practices. She'd found a role where her character was an ASL interpreter in a movie set to film in March. A deaf teenage actress would play the lead ever so much better than a hearing actress pretending to be deaf.

Andrew was in the process of qualifying for a national interpreter's license, which would come in handy as Hastings's newest client was deaf and would be in the same movie as Jordan. Instead of leaving the family business, Andrew started a West Coast office.

Maria touched up Jordan's makeup. "There. Perfect. I'm so glad I could see you again."

"Are you staying?"

"No, I wanted the seats to go to someone who appreciates sign language, but I'll watch from home."

Jordan stood and smoothed her black dress. "I still can't believe Hearthfire is live-streaming it on their website." According to social media posts deaf teens and parents across the country planned to watch the video stream.

"You're ready. Go break a leg." Maria closed her lipstick jar.

"You are taking the job as my personal artist, right?"

"Turned in my notice to Hearthfire this morning."

Jordan gave Maria a hug before joining the others in the wings.

Andrew stood behind her, wrapping his arms around her waist. "I can't believe you talked me into acting."

Jordan leaned into his hug, one of her favorite places to be. "Technically, you are interpreting."

"But the kissing scenes…"

"We don't have to do those. We are interpreting, not acting. Although with you, I don't need to act like I did with Storm."

Andrew nuzzled her neck. "Good."

A light near the stage turned from red to yellow letting everyone know they had thirty seconds till curtain. Andrew let Jordan go and went to stand on his mark. He wouldn't appear until the second scene.

Jordan and the interpreter playing Reggie's role walked out on stage.

An hour and twenty-seven minutes later, the stage was cleared of everyone but Jordan and Andrew.

"Princess, we need to talk," signed Andrew in sync with Storm's voice.

"Why?"

"Because I have come to several conclusions. The most important is that I love you."

"Really?" Not for the first time, Jordan wondered at the script-writer's skills.

Andrew dropped to one knee and pulled out a ring box, balancing it on his knee. Above her, the screen went dark. This was not what they had practiced.

"Yes, Jordan Lee." Andrew spoke as he signed. "Marry me?"

Jordan covered her mouth with her hands, tears streaming from her eyes. She nodded, then nodded again.

"I'm not sure our audience caught your answer."

Jordan turned to the audience and fisted both hands, signing a double yes. Andrew stood and pulled Jordan into a movie-worthy kiss.

The interpreter actor playing the part of the king came out and shouted as he signed, "And they lived happily ever after."

Following a ten-minute intermission, they finished the last act of the show, ending with the wedding. Jordan kissed Andrew in a much more realistic kiss than the one playing above their heads. She vowed that the real wedding scene would be even better and that her dress wouldn't have a train at all—so Princess couldn't try to chew it.

acknowledgements

WE ADOPTED SNOOPY FROM AN animal shelter in 2013. Somewhere along the way he became very attached to me. It's a rare day when I write that he doesn't try to share my lap with my computer. I used many of his traits and his coloring to inspire Princess.

Thank you Lee for letting me use your name! The name Jet appears in this book as Janet N. supported a great cause and chose a name for this book.

As always, thanks to Tammy, Nanette and Cami who are so willing to help make all my projects better and to read for all my mistakes. I would never make it through a day without Sally and Cindy whose advice keeps me going. Thank you wonderful ladies.

Michele at Eschler Editing does the best edits; any mistakes left in this book are not her fault. Nor are my excellent proofreaders to be blamed. Thank you ladies and gents!

My family, for sharing their home with the fictional characters who often got fed better than they did. And my husband who encourages me every crazy step of the way and puts up with all my messy spreadsheets.

And to my Father in Heaven for putting these wonderful people, and any I may have forgotten to mention, in my life. I am grateful for every experience and blessing I have been granted.

about the author

LORIN GRACE WAS BORN IN Colorado and has been moving around the country ever since, living in eight states and several imaginary worlds. She graduated from Brigham Young University with a degree in Graphic Design.

Currently, she lives in northern Utah with her husband, four children, and a dog who is insanely jealous of her laptop. When not writing, Lorin enjoys creating graphics, visiting historical sites, museums, and reading.

Lorin is an active member of the League of Utah Writers and was awarded Honorable Mention in their 2016 creative writing contest short romance story category. Her debut novel, *Waking Lucy,* was awarded a 2017 Recommended Read award in the LUW Published book contest. In 2018 Mending Fences with the Billionaire, also received a Recommended Read award.

You can learn more about her, and sign up for her newsletter at loringrace.com or at Facebook: LorinGraceWriter.